Other publications by
Fletcher Books:

Out West and Back

The Panther on Cold Mountain and Other Stories

Little Sam Mountain

Little Sam Mountain — The Journey

The Sheriff

Grassy Top Mountain

Little Sam Mountain — Living Their Dream

Forks of the Pigeon

These books are available from Ingram, Amazon.com,
Baker & Taylor, Barnes & Noble, and directly from the author.

Charles C. Fletcher
2310 Harris Circle NW
Cleveland, TN 37311
423-476-6835
ccfletch9@yahoo.com

Memories from Thickety

by T.P. Fletcher

Published By
Fletcher Books
2310 Harris Circle NW
Cleveland, TN 37311

Memories from Thickety

Copyright © 2014 by Talmadge P. Fletcher

All rights reserved. No part of this book may be reproduced, stored in a retrieval system, or transmitted in any form or by any means without the prior written permission of the publisher, except by a reviewer who may quote brief passages in a review to be printed in a newspaper, magazine, or journal.

ISBN: 978-1-4951-0485-5
Published by Fletcher Books
2310 Harris Circle NW
Cleveland, TN, 37311

Printed in the United States of America

Contents

Preface vii
My Early Years 1
My Early School Years 13
My Later School Years 45
Drafted 71
World War II 97
Married 127
Civilian Life 141
Family 153
Retirement 173
My Family Tree 185
Photo Gallery 187
Acknowledgements 201

Preface

For the last several years, my granddaughter, Amy DeWeese, has wanted me to write a book telling about the things that happened to me during my lifetime. I am not a writer, but I will try to describe what it was like living during the Great Depression, World War II, and the years following. I have been blessed with a life of ninety years and a loving family, and I want the younger people of today to know about what I experienced.

Some of the stories in this book were told to me by my mother and some by my brother, Charles. My mother is no longer with us, but Charles still helps me with the stories about things we both encountered during the early years of our lives.

Some of the things in my life were hardships, but as I look back I can see a bit of humor in them. By reading these stories I hope the younger generations will learn what a difference there is between today and what we call "the good old days." In those days we didn't have a washing machine, a refrigerator, an electric stove, a TV, a radio, a car, or several other things that depend on electricity because we didn't have electricity. We never missed those things because we never had them.

The stories in this book are mostly ones that only I know about now. I want to preserve this personal history for my children, my grandchildren, and my other kin. I also would like for my readers to ponder what they would have done had they been in my shoes (or walking in my bare feet).

Memories from Thickety

My Early Years

Gastonia, North Carolina

It was a cold night in December of 1927 when my mother, Margaret Ellen Fletcher, was awakened to the smell of smoke. Realizing that the house was in flames, her first thought was to get me, my older brother, Charles, and my baby sister, Louise, out of the burning house. She ran to the room where we were sleeping and got us out safely. She awakened the neighbors and asked them to call the fire department, but the man next door said he didn't have time because he was trying to keep his own house from catching fire. Mother then asked the neighbor on the other side of our house, and that neighbor called the fire department. By the time they arrived, the house was completely engulfed in flames, and it was too late to save anything, except a fireproof trunk that held some family pictures and a few keepsakes, but they were scorched.

My father, who was working within sight of our house, heard that a house was on fire, and he saw that it was ours. He left his job at the Firestone Cotton Mill and rushed home to find that we were cold but safe, and he realized there was nothing he could do to save the house and our belongings. One of the firemen told him that a policeman had knocked through a screened window to see if there was anyone left in the burning house.

We were thankful that the Lord had saved us from a fiery death. We were also thankful that my dad's mother, who operated a boarding house close by, took us in until we could decide what to do. We were all wearing only our night clothes and were barefoot. So, we were told to stay in bed until the stores opened the next day when my parents could buy us some clothes.

Let me give you a little background. I was born at 214 King Street, Gastonia, North Carolina, on October 28th, 1923. My father, Dewey Talmadge Fletcher, worked at the Firestone Cotton Mill, and we rented the house on King Street from the mill. The house that I was born in was not the same house that burned — in fact, with a little bit of remodeling done since then, the house on King Street is still there today. We moved to the house that burned later on, so that my dad could walk to work.

My father was born in Haywood County, North Carolina, on December 13th, 1900. My mother was born on April 1st, 1905, in the same county. They were married on June 12th, 1921. My brother Charles was born on Trenton Street in Gastonia on April 1st, 1922; my older sister, Louise, was born in Cramerton, North Carolina, on June 20th, 1926; and my younger sister, Leveta, was born in Canton, North Carolina, on January 9th, 1931.

At this time my grandfather, Charlie Pressley, was farming in Greeley, Colorado. He had spent most of his life in Haywood County, North Carolina, on a farm located in the Stamey Cove community, which was about three miles from Canton. He had a hard life trying to make a living while raising eight children. He and Grandma worked hard at raising tobacco and corn. They had a large farm, but it was mostly mountain land, and the yield was small. My mother helped all she could on the farm. When my mother was ten years old, she and her family moved to Greeley, Colorado, where Grandpa thought he could make a better living on a 160-acre rented farm. They stayed there a few years and were able to make a good living.

When Mama was fourteen years old, she begged Grandpa to move back to Canton. She was at the age when girls started looking at boys, and she couldn't see any she liked out in the country where they lived. Finally, Grandpa moved the family back to Canton, and when Mama was sixteen years old, she met my dad, and they were married. They lived in Gastonia, North Carolina, where Charles, Louise, and I were born, and we were living there when our house burned down.

When Grandpa got a letter from my mother telling him about the fire, he told us to come out there and help him on his 160-acre farm. He grew sugar beets, along with beans and other crops. Mama had lived there, along with her sister and five brothers, already once. When her family moved back to North Carolina, her father had been able to buy his old farm back, but the family only stayed a few years before they moved back to Colorado. My mom had stayed in Canton after she got married. After my mom persuaded my dad to go out west, Grandpa sent money for train tickets so that we could move to Colorado.

After staying four weeks with Grandma Fletcher, who hated to see us go, we packed up, including food that wouldn't spoil (since we couldn't afford the high prices in the dining car), and prepared to leave. Charles and I were thrilled to ride on a train. We had watched trains go through Gastonia many times, never thinking we would someday get to ride on one.

Greeley, Colorado

When it was time to board the train, the conductor called out in his loudest voice, "All aboard!" and we got on board and found our seats. We were looking forward to both our first train ride and to seeing our Grandma and Grandpa. We didn't eat very much during the trip, but we didn't starve either — we were too busy looking out the window and watching the mountains change to flat land, then back to mountains again to worry much about eating.

The ride was an adventure for us, and it gave us something to talk about while we were traveling. We didn't have money to ride in the sleeping car, so when night came, we curled up in our seats and slept, dreaming of what it would be like when we got to Colorado. After a couple of days, though, we became anxious to finish the trip and get to Grandpa's farm.

When the train arrived in Denver, one of our uncles met us and took us to see the rest of the family. We had a happy reunion when we arrived, and we prepared to start a new life.

We stayed in Greeley for about two years. Every able-bodied person worked hard in order to make a good crop that would sell in the market. Grandpa and all of his five boys already had worked there for several profitable years.

The crops were planted in long rows, and in the hot, dry weather, the sugar beets and other crops needed a lot of water. Irrigation ditches were used to supply water, and when the ditches were full, we children were tempted to play in them. After seeing where we wanted to play, one day my dad decided to use drastic measures to keep us out of the water. He took rope and tied my brother, Charles, and me to the bed and left us there while everyone else was helping with the farm work.

After an hour or two, we talked our three year old sister, Louise, into getting us a knife from the kitchen. She brought us a large butcher knife, which we used to cut ourselves loose. We then went outside, but we stayed away from the water and obeyed our parents so we wouldn't get tied up again.

We spent a lot of time exploring around the farm. We were glad to see things that we weren't used to seeing in cotton mill country. My Uncle Clifford showed us things that they had to do in order to produce good crops. He was about ten years old, and we thought he was the smartest "man" around, and we believed everything he told us.

One summer while we were there, a storm forced us into a storm-cellar for safety. They called it a "cyclone", but we had always called that type of storm a "tornado." Almost everyone had a shelter dug out under their house to go into during these storms. Every storm that passed didn't cause damage, but on this occasion the roof blew off the barn.

Although there was no other damage to the farm, it was around this time that the Great Depression hit world-wide. All of a sudden, the farmers couldn't sell to the merchants, because the merchants had no buyers. At this point, we decided to go back to North Carolina.

We didn't have much money, and we sold everything that we could to get some cash. Dad even took our milk cow to town and traded it for a Model T Ford car. The old car had to have the clutch and brake shoes lined pretty often, and flat tires were a common occurrence. So, Dad got a good supply of brake and clutch shoes, along with patching glue and patching rubber, to prepare for our trip. Mom cooked several pheasants that Dad had killed, and she dressed several chickens and packed them in ice (which was plentiful at that time of year). We packed lots of potatoes, pinto beans, and anything else that could be cooked alongside the road, and we headed back east.

After three days on the road, we ran out of chicken, and we began eating lots of beans and potatoes. As we slowly went on our way, we traded our belongings for something to eat. Dad had a good suit, and he sold it for five dollars to buy food. I don't know all of the details, but my mother told me that somehow she got us turned around, and it cost us about 500 extra miles of traveling, something we surely didn't need.

We ran out of money in Arkansas. Dad wired his mother, and she sent us enough money to get us home to North Carolina. We had to wait for the money, and during this time my dad couldn't find work. Jobs were scarce because people everywhere were feeling the results of the Great Depression. With the help of the Lord, we made it to my Great-

Aunt Grace Smathers' home in Canton, North Carolina, arriving in the middle of the night. That is one trip I wouldn't want to take again.

Canton, North Carolina

After breakfast the next day, Aunt Grace wanted to sit down and hear all about our trip to Colorado and back, and she wanted to know what life was like on the big farm. She said she couldn't imagine what it was like, almost starving on a diet of potatoes.

Aunt Grace was a widow, but she had a stepdaughter to help her make a garden, so she always had a can-house full of vegetables and canned meats. No one ever left her house hungry.

While we told Aunt Grace about our adventures, my dad went to look for a house and a job. He was lucky, because he got a job in the paper mill in Canton and found a house near Aunt Grace. I'm not sure how we obtained furniture, but we moved in and were happy to settle down near our Aunt Grace.

A few days ago, I passed the old house, and I marveled that it is still there, eighty-five years later. Although it is empty and the lot around it is all grown up in weeds, the house is still standing. I doubt if it will ever have anyone rent it now. It served its purpose at the time we lived in it, but things are different now, and most people want a larger house with all the modern conveniences. When I pass it now, I still think back to the time we were lucky to call it home, back in the year 1929.

I remember one time later when I went to Aunt Grace's to spend the night. When we ate supper, we had the best pinto beans that I had ever tasted. When she asked what I wanted for breakfast, I told her I wanted some more of those beans. She told me they wouldn't be good for breakfast, but if I wanted some that is what she would give me. Aunt Grace was right; they were not good for breakfast. I always liked to be at her house when she made hominy. I always got enough to fill me up by taking samples.

When Aunt Grace saw me coming, she would wipe the snuff off her mouth with her apron and kiss me. All of the women wore aprons as part of their dress back then. Aunt Grace was happy when someone came to visit, more so when a young person came to stay all night. She always tried to make anyone welcome. When bed time came, she made me take a spoonful of a mixture of aloes and vinegar. (I think that was what it was, anyway.) It sure didn't taste good, but she made up for it at breakfast. The only thing I didn't like about those visits was being kissed.

One time when I was much older, when Grandma Fletcher's third husband, Mr. Worley, died (she always called him "Mr. Worley"), Aunt Grace and her sister, Beulah Henson, wanted me to take them to Gastonia to visit and offer condolences. When I picked them up, they both were really dressed up in their best aprons. When we were coming back home, they wanted to stop at a pottery store. I found out why when we got there; the man who ran the place did not have any arms, and both Aunt Grace and Aunt Beulah bought something just to watch the man make change with his feet. I really enjoyed that trip.

My Early School Years

Near where we were living was an old building which was used for both a church and a school house. That was the place where I first went to school. It was located in the community called (at that time) Austin Ridge, and it was on a steep road that went over a place called Smathers Hill. Those who owned a car would try it out there and brag about what gear it took to climb the hill.

I was a little boy, happy to start school in the first week of September. However, my happiness didn't last long. When the school found out I was only five years old, they sent me home to wait until next year.

After a long year of waiting, I finally got to go to school. By this time, the school had moved to the North Canton School, and we got to ride a school bus. This didn't last but about six weeks, though, before we had to transfer to the newly-built school in the Beaverdam community, closer to home. I wanted to stay at the North Canton School because I had made friends there, but I had to transfer.

I already hated that new school before I ever went. The first day, I hid when I saw the bus coming. But, Mama saw me and carried me to the bus that morning. After that day, I was too ashamed to be seen being carried by my mother again, so I got on the bus. I soon found new friends at the school, and I started to like it better.

The school was built where there had been a grove of trees, so there were a lot of stumps left behind from the cut-down trees. Discipline was strict, and when the larger boys did something wrong, they were given a stump to dig up for punishment. All of this had to be done after school hours. Once, one of the older boys had been given a stump to remove, and after everyone was gone, he went home and got some dynamite to blast out his stump. When the principal found out, the boy was then given two more stumps to dig up.

One morning as students were getting off the school bus, rocks, splinters of stump, and dirt came showering down all over the bus. The boy had blown up another stump. To the best of my memory, by the time school let out for the summer, that boy still had seven more stumps to dig out. I don't know if he ever got them out or not.

Everyone who misbehaved didn't have to dig stumps. Some were whipped with a rubber hose in the principal's office. Word got around, and most everyone was sure not to get punished in that manner. After I settled into the school with new friends, I really liked it there. I remember my first year's report card had nothing but Bs on it.

We moved again that year, but within the same community, so I didn't have to switch schools. We moved into an old log house that belonged to a Mr. Smathers. The house was below a graveyard and close to a big spring that had good water, and we were able to walk to school from it. It had a loft where my brother and I slept. We had to climb a wall-mounted ladder to get up there, and we slept on straw-tick mattresses. When it snowed, the snow would blow through the cracks and leave little ridges of snow inside. We survived by "scrooching" together to keep warm.

Charles and I had the job of gathering wood for the cook-stove and the old fireplace. Mr. Smathers gave us all the wood we could drag into the house — dead limbs that Charles and I could gather, plus what we could chop or saw with a crosscut saw. Charles and I also had the chore of getting up early and starting fires in the cook-stove and fireplace.

We would take turns at getting up at 4:00 AM and making the fires. We made sure we got the best kindling we could find to build the fires.

One of my other chores was to milk a cow. She was gentle enough to milk from both sides. She gave more milk than I could carry, so Mama carried it to the house for me. Charles and I were told to do things only once, and we learned how to work. That lesson has served me well throughout my lifetime.

One Sunday while we lived in that house, Mama wanted to go visit Grandpa Pressley, her father. She took our sister Louise and left Charles, Dad, and me at home. I don't know if it was pre-arranged, but soon after Mama left, a man I'll call "Jack" showed up at our house with some whisky. It wasn't long before Jack and Dad got drunk, and Dad traded our cow, the best milker in town, for a cow that he had never seen.

I don't know how Jack knew about us having that good cow, and I don't believe that he was as drunk as he acted. Dad sent Charles and me to go with Jack and bring that sorry old cow back, and when I went to milk her, she didn't have but a little milk. I could carry it all myself.

When Mama got home and saw what had happened, she really gave Dad a piece of her mind (not only that day, but for the whole next week). When Sunday came, she went back to Grandpa's again and told my dad that he had better have her cow back when she returned. I don't know how Dad got Jack to come to our house again, but he came. (Maybe there was a promise of moonshine.) That day, Jack and Dad made another trade, and Jack was the sorry one that time. Jack traded our cow back for the one we got from him the week before, but we had to give him one of our pigs, to boot (extra).

The pig weighed about thirty pounds, and they put it in a sack. Charles and I went with Jack to bring our cow back home. When we got about a half mile up the road, Jack's son, who was carrying the pig, told Jack it had quit kicking. Jack told him to open up the sack and give the pig some air, but it was too late — the pig was dead. Jack said, "It's all right. Put him back in the sack."

It was about two miles to where Jack lived, and when the pig was dumped out of the sack, it was really dead. Jack's son asked his dad what he wanted him to do with the dead pig, and Jack said, "Take the pig down to the barn. We'll eat him for supper." All of this trading cost us a lot of trouble, a pig, and all of the scolding that Mama gave our dad.

We moved so often, it is hard for me to remember every home in chronological order. At one time, we lived in a house on Cross Road Hill in a place that we called "Home Brew Knob." It was called that because the people who lived across the road were said to be bootleggers. They were the people who we rented from.

We had to get our water from a one-hundred foot deep well across the road, and every Monday it was my job to draw water for washing using a bucket and a windlass. It took a long while for me to get enough water to wash clothes.

That winter it snowed several inches deep, and then it got cold enough to freeze hard enough to ride downhill on almost anything you could stay on. That freeze gave us some good rides on the long sloping pasture close to where the North Canton Baptist Church is now. The freeze came to an end a day or two later when the sun came out and thawed the ice and snow. The pasture was scattered with pasteboard boxes, straight backed chairs, a few homemade sleds, and a few store bought sleds.

The woman who owned the house we lived in got mad at my mother and threatened to not let us get water from the well. So, we moved to another house, where my younger sister, Leveta, was born. While we lived at our new location, we never missed school or failed to do our chores, although going to school and doing chores together did make for a long day.

After we moved, my Uncle Doyle rented the previous house we had lived in. One day Charles, a boy named Bill Fletcher (not related), and I were walking through the woods below that house. One of us (I don't remember which one) kicked into a pile of sawdust, and out came a half-gallon jar of moonshine. While we were looking at it, a man came out of the house onto the porch and hollered at us to put it down; but, instead, we ran away with it. Charles and Bill then temporarily became bootleggers because they sold the moonshine to someone for fifty cents. We later found out that Uncle Doyle was selling moonshine from that house, and he found out that it was us who took that half-gallon.

While we were living there, we got to be friends with the family who lived across the road, the Reed family. They had moved to Canton from Alabama. They had three boys and a girl. The oldest boy, James, was my best friend, and one of the other boys, Edwin, was my brother's friend. We played games, climbed trees, played marbles, and did anything else we could think of for fun.

Mr. Reed smoked cigarettes, and one day Edwin got a pack, and James, my brother, and I went out behind the barn and smoked the whole pack. I don't think that Mr. Reed missed the cigarettes, but when Edwin took his dad's cigars later on, he had to face a whipping.

One day, James and I were playing marbles with acorns (we didn't have marbles), and James got mad and stepped on my acorns, causing a fight. James went home and told his dad that I started the fight, but his dad had been watching us and knew James had started the fight. Thankfully, that didn't ruin our friendship.

Later on, when we were living in West Canton, I would wade the Pigeon River to go visit him. Also, while we were in high school, we both worked for Mr. Scaggs after school on Friday and Saturday. He was building a combination store and gas station. He and his family — Ernest, Mrs. Scaggs, and son Teddy — were from Pennsylvania. They wanted to go back to Pennsylvania for a week and wanted James and me to look after their place, which we did. James did the milking, and I cooked breakfast and washed the dishes, and we caught the school bus and went to school. We were housekeepers for a week while they visited their kinfolk.

That summer, one day after we had gone to bed, Mama's brother came to the house and woke us up. He had been hauling moonshine, and he got word that the Sheriff was waiting to catch him. He had gone by the mill where my dad was working and told him the Law was waiting at a place he was going to pass through. He took another road, and he asked to bring the load to our house until the next day.

Dad didn't want his brother-in-law to get caught, so he agreed. Mama didn't like it, but she didn't want her brother to go to jail, so she got me and Charles to help him hide the moonshine in our cornfield. The moon was shining bright, and we dug holes and buried it, all except one case of half gallons, which we buried in a hog lot down below our spring. Not long after it was buried, the Sheriff came with a search warrant to search our house. He didn't find anything, though, and he left believing someone had told him a lie.

The next day, our uncle came to get his moonshine, and Charles and I went with him to dig it up. We hid it pretty well because it was hard to find. In fact, we never did find one box of it. However, we didn't have any trouble finding what we hid in the hog lot, for our old sow had dug it up, broken a jar, and gotten drunk on it.

While my uncle was trying to salvage what jars were not broken, the old sow got out of the lot. When we tried to get her back in, we had a terrible time getting the old drunk sow back into the lot. Several years later while I was working in Baltimore, Maryland, I saw a drunken woman who reminded me of that old drunk sow.

I remember another thing that happened to another uncle. I had gone to Grandpa's to spend the night. It was Saturday, and Uncle Clifford asked if I wanted to go to the movies. I said I didn't have any money, and he said he would pay my way. We headed to town, and when we came to a store, Clifford said he had to stop. We went into the store, and Uncle Clifford bought a pound of coffee and paid for it with a five dollar bill. The man asked where he got that five dollars, and Clifford answered that his papa gave it to him to buy coffee, and that he was allowed to use the rest of the money to go to the picture show.

We went to the theater and had to wait for it to open. While we were standing there waiting, Clifford was counting his money, and he dropped two dollars. A man who was walking by picked up the money and walked away. One of the boys waiting there told Clifford that the man was a certain lawyer in town.

Clifford and I followed the man to his office and told him to give us back our money. The man said he didn't have our money. Clifford said, "When I tell Papa, he will come here, and you'll give it to him."

We went back to Grandpa's and told him what had happened. At that point, Clifford confessed to him that he had stolen the money from Aunt Charlotte, who was working at the Enka textile mill. (She was not married at the time.) Grandpa went to see the lawyer, and he got the money back. Clifford and I never went to the show. Instead, Clifford went home with me and stayed all night.

I went to Grandpa's every chance I got and stayed as long as Mama would let me. I always enjoyed watching Grandpa while he was stirring the gravy that he and his family ate for breakfast every morning. Grandpa was good to me, and I would go with him wherever he went. When Grandpa got a new hat, he would give me his old one, and I would finish wearing it out.

One time Grandpa went up on the mountain while we were living in his house (after Uncle Fred had moved) to plant corn in a plot of "new ground" that had never been planted. Charles, Clifford, and I went with him to help. We accompanied Grandpa while he did most of the work (if not all of it).

When we stopped to eat the lunch that Grandma had fixed for us, Charles and Clifford were watching a young calf. They decided they were cowboys, and they got some old cords off a scarecrow and crossed over a fence to catch the calf and ride it. They never were successful, but they tried, and their cowboy days were soon over.

Another time when I went to stay a few days with Grandpa, he was making twists out of his tobacco. He and some of my uncles chewed the tobacco twists that he made, and Uncle Alva crumbled it and smoked it in his pipe. It sure had a strong taste when it was chewed, and it emitted a strong odor when it was smoked in a pipe. My Grandma didn't chew it, but she did chew apple-flavored plug tobacco. A lot of the women in that region dipped snuff, and they usually kept a twig of a black gum tree to use for a toothbrush.

I kept watching Grandpa that day, and finally I told him I would like to have a chew. Grandpa said that it might make me sick, but I said I didn't believe it would. He gave me some of his tobacco twist, and I didn't know not to swallow it. It wasn't long before I was sick, and Grandma put me to bed until I got over it. Grandpa was right (as usual).

That day I was cured from wanting to chew that old burley tobacco.

Another thing I watched Grandpa do was feed his pigs. He always had a white pig that had a lot of fat in the meat. He would take a big bucket of feed and watch the pigs eat until everything was all gone. After his pigs were killed and dressed, he would cook a big piece of fat. Grandpa would eat all of the fat instead of the lean meat.

During the Presidential campaign in the early years of the Depression, when President Hoover was being challenged by Franklin Roosevelt, all of my uncles were Democrats. They brought a lot of posters with the Democrats' pictures on them and put them all over the house. Grandpa, who was a Republican, tore the posters down as fast as they were put up. After the election, (Roosevelt won in a landslide victory, with 472 electoral votes versus 59 for Hoover), the Public Works Administration (PWA) was started, and all of the boys got jobs. Grandpa was a Democrat from then on.

Near Christmastime, one of the men who lived in the community wanted my dad to help him earn a little money for Christmas. (I won't mention the man's name.) He wanted Dad to drive his car (we didn't have one) to go get a load of whiskey. The plan was that they would sell it and split the money, and it wasn't hard to talk Dad into it. He drove the man's car, and while he was coming back with the car full of moonshine, the Law was waiting for him, stopped him, and put him in jail.

The man who owned the car came to our house and asked if Dad had come back with the car that he had loaned him. He didn't tell Mama where Dad had gone. He came two or three times to see if Dad had come back. Eventually, he got worried, and he went to town and reported that his car had been stolen. When Dad got out of jail, he was charged with stealing the man's car, and he was going to be tried both for stealing the car and hauling whiskey. When he realized he was going to jail, he fled to Colorado and stayed gone for two years.

Grandpa Pressley helped us all he could. He found us a place to live. It was an old house in the West Canton community of Phillipsville called "the old Johnson place." Fred Pace, who was living in a house that Grandpa owned, moved into another house nearby where he could have a paint shop, and we moved into that house and didn't have to pay rent.

Uncle Fred was married to Aunt Charlotte, my mother's sister. I sometimes spent the night with them. One time when I stayed overnight with them, I got out of bed and was sleep-walking. Aunt Charlotte said I came into her room and got hold of her big toe. She told me, "My toe just came off, and now I will have to put it back on!"

Another time I stayed all night, and the next day, the man next-door wanted me to mow his yard. That was before they started making lawn-mowers with gasoline powered engines. The grass was pretty high, and it took me most of the day to get it mowed. The man gave me twenty-five cents for my work. I surely earned that quarter.

Sometime later, I remember when Uncle Fred had several of the neighbors visiting, someone said, "If we had a chicken, we could have a chicken stew."

Vernon, one of my mother's brothers, said, "I`ve got some chickens, and I'll go get one of them." However, what he had in mind was to get one of his brother's chickens. It was dark, and he got a big fat hen and brought it back. It made plenty of stew for everyone. The next day Vernon counted his chickens and found one was missing. In the dark, he had stolen one of his own chickens, thinking it was one of Uncle Clifford's.

Uncles Clifford and Vern wanted to take me snipe hunting one time. I asked them, "What is a snipe?"

They told me, "It is a kind of bird that only gets out at night, and you catch them in a sack."

They went on to explain that one person had to hold the sack, and the other two would go down through the corn field and flush out the snipes, and then those two would run the snipes up toward the person who was holding the sack so he could catch them. I was chosen to be the sack holder. I didn't know what was up, but by the way it was explained to me, I smelled a rat. I told them that holding the bag was the easy part, but they convinced me that it was the most important job, and that I could do a better job than they could.

I said, "OK, but I still think one of you could do it better."

They gave me the sack and said, "You sort-of hunker down and be sure to watch for them — and don't worry, they won't bite you."

The moon was bright that night, and I watched my uncles go down the corn rows. When I thought they wouldn't see me, I slipped up to Uncle Fred's and told him what was going on, and he got a big laugh out of it. He explained that there was no such thing as a snipe, and that they wanted to see how long I would stay there holding the sack. When Vern and Clifford thought they could go back to the house without being seen, they came into Uncle Fred's (thinking I was still holding the sack) and were laughing about it, talking about how long I would hold the sack. I came out of hiding and told them that I got the sack full and came on back to the house. The joke was on them that night.

Moving to this house meant we had to change to the Patton School, named for the Patton family, who owned most of the land on that side of town. I liked school there. I had a good teacher in the fourth grade, Mr. Williams, who taught me well. I don't know if I ever had a better teacher in my early years, and I still remember some of the things he taught me.

While we were living there, I got acquainted with a boy in the neighborhood who had a tame rabbit and a dog. One day while he was playing with the rabbit, the dog got hold of it and killed the rabbit. In his anger, the boy killed his dog as punishment for killing his rabbit. It reminds me of an old lady who had two matches, and when she lost one, she struck the other to help her find the one she lost. Also, once I watched a man who just bought a new screen door install it. Something went wrong, and he took his hammer and destroyed the screen because he was mad. As the old saying goes, "Some people will cut off their nose to spite their face."

When the walnuts were matured and falling off the trees across the river from Grandpa's, I would get Letch Hall to take me across in a boat to where I could gather them. I would gather a pile and take the hulls off them, and then I would spread them out to dry and call for Letch to come get me. Sometimes he didn't hear me for a long time, but eventually he would come get me before dark.

After several days, when I thought I had enough walnuts dried out, I brought them back from across the river. The best I remember, someone gave me two dollars for them, and I gave the money to Mama to help with household expenses. The money helped a lot. My hands were brown from hulling, but the stain finally came off. From that day until now, I have always enjoyed gathering walnuts. After I was married, my wife would help me pick the meat out of them, and we used them in baking cakes, pies, and other things. Walnuts flavored them with a good taste.

I remember having one roller-skate, which I could ride down an old broken sidewalk. I couldn't stop until I got to the bottom of the hill, where the sidewalk ended, at which point I would jump off and roll into the dirt and gravel road. I visited that old place a few years ago, and it looked like it did when we lived there, but the old house was gone. We moved again that year, but we didn't have to change to another school that time.

We later moved into a house in the Mingus Cove. There was a man who lived across the road who had broken his back, and he had to walk bowed over. He shined shoes in a barber shop for a living. When he came home each evening, he would bring home a cross-tie that the railroad gave away after they repaired their tracks. When he had several cross-ties, he would get me and Charles to saw the ties up for stove wood.

We would saw the cross-ties up on Saturday morning. When we got them all sawed up, we would go to our house and take a bath. Then we would go to the barber shop where the man worked, and he would give each of us a quarter. We then would go to the Haywood Café and buy two hot dogs and a big Coke, which cost us fifteen cents each. We took the dime that we had left and went to the movies, where they always had a western, and we watched it two times. That was a well-spent Saturday for us.

While we lived in Mingus Cove, someone from the nearby Baptist church wanted to have a prayer meeting at our house. We couldn't refuse them, and a house-full of people showed up for prayer meeting. Charles and I went on to bed early.

Once the prayer meeting really got going, someone started shouting, and the rest of the attendees started to follow along. When everybody had joined in the shouting, people started jumping up and down, and one corner of the house came off the foundation and fell to the ground. That broke up the prayer meeting, and everyone went home. The next day, the house had to be jacked up and put back on the locust pole that held up that corner of the house, at least when no one was jumping and shouting inside.

One day that summer when school was out, I went blackberry-picking up on the mountain above where we lived. My friend James Reed went with me, and by the time we got our buckets full we were on the other side of the mountain. As we were going down to the road, we came upon a boy who had built a shelter out of bark. It had started raining, and he was trying to build a fire. When we came by, he wanted us to go to a house nearby and get him some matches. He was a lot older than us, and he told us that he told his mama he would not be home again until he got his bucket full. Since it wasn't full, I guess he was going to stay all night. The last time I heard of him, he was in Tennessee.

There was a boy who lived in West Canton who was always in trouble at home. Sometimes, he would leave home and come to our house and spend the night. When we went to school, we took a short-cut, and one morning on the way to school, all of a sudden, he knocked Charles down. I didn't see Charles do anything to him. He was a mean boy, and we were afraid of him. He was a lot older than we were. One day after school, he wanted me to take a fifty-cent piece to Allen's Store and buy a nickel's worth of candy. He said I could have half. I asked, "Where did you get fifty cents?" and he told me that he found it in a book at school.

When Mr. Allen saw the coin, he asked, "Where did you get this?" and I told him. He told me that the coin was made out of lead. I think he had seen that boy before. Later on, after the boy was grown, he was put in prison. I saw him on TV with a group of convicts. Growing up in our lifetime was a battle which was sometimes the "survival of the fittest."

When my dad decided to come home and face his trial, he had to hobo trains to get back. When he got home, he turned himself in and was tried for the moonshine haul. The man from Canton had dropped the stolen car charge by then. During the trial, the man kept telling Dad not to mention his name, and he would help him pay the fine, but he never tried to help. When they were going to give Dad two years in prison, he told them what had happened. They had a new trial, and when Mama got on the stand and told how the man had come to the house and loaned his car to Dad, they gave the man a fine of $750. When he begged for a lesser amount, the fine was dropped to $500, and the Judge told him if he asked for less, he would send him to prison. Dad was fined $62.10.

After the trial, Dad got his job back at the paper mill, and we moved back to the Beaverdam community, and I went back to the Beaverdam School for fifth grade. I had a good teacher that year, too. Every morning we sang a hymn before class started, and we had class spelling bees, which I enjoyed. School sure has changed since then.

My Grandma Pressley had a brother, Wilson Putnam, who lived in the Stamey Cove section of Haywood County. He had a large farm with cattle, and he grew a large tobacco patch. When I was allowed to spend a few days with him, I was happy.

I would walk across the mountain by myself — I wasn't afraid. Uncle Wilson was a widower who had two boys and two girls who were grown but unmarried at that time. When I went to visit, they treated me as if I was family (or better). The girls would treat me as if I belonged to them, and they would fix me anything to eat that I wanted. When night came, I was put into the best featherbed, where I would really stay warm. It was lot better than a straw-tick mattress. When morning came, the girls would fix me a breakfast of ham and eggs with hot biscuits and lots of honey that came from the bee hives on their farm.

After breakfast, Uncle Wilson would let me follow him and let me help if there was something I could do. If he had tobacco that needed the worms picked off, I could do that. I don't believe I have ever seen such an ugly worm as the one that you find on tobacco, but I got them off. Now the farmers spray the tobacco with a spray that kills them. Uncle Wilson also let me watch him rob the bee hives of honey. I didn't get too close, for I didn't want to be stung. He was not afraid, but he did have a hat with a veil over his face. I learned a lot of things about farming from him that helped me make a garden after I grew up.

I also learned what it takes to go fox hunting from him. One time while I was visiting Uncle Wilson, he thought I was old enough and big enough to go fox hunting. I don't know if I had ever wanted to go, but I was willing to go. He had some old hounds that each had a name. When it was dark, he put them on a leash, and away we went. He had a regular hunting buddy, and he brought his dogs too, and I thought there were enough dogs to catch anything. I didn't know that all the men wanted to do was to listen to the dogs bark while they chased foxes. They seemed to know the voice of each dog. When they decided it was time to go back down the mountain, I was glad, and I never went fox hunting at night with Uncle Wilson again.

Later on, we went hunting in the daytime and tried to kill foxes for their hide, but I don't remember ever killing but one. We didn't have a fox hound, and the regular fox hunters wouldn't let us use their dogs.

I visited Uncle Wilson several times and enjoyed each visit. I went to visit him after I got out of the Army, and he was all alone. The girls were married and gone. I don't know how his son, Arthur, died or the girls, but his son, Don, was killed in a tragic accident. He was married, and he worked at the paper mill. One day he was going home from work, and he stopped to change a flat tire. While he was changing it, he left his lights on, and an oncoming driver, blinded by the lights, couldn't help hitting him, and he was killed instantly.

Gastonia Again

We didn't stay in one place very long when I was a child. After school was out, we moved back Gastonia, North Carolina. This time we moved into an apartment in West Gastonia that was over a drug store. We didn't like it there, but we had to stay while we looked for a house to rent.

I started to school in the sixth grade that year, and the only thing I liked was a great big pecan tree that was along the path to school. I used to fill my pockets with nuts on the way to school and on the way back home.

When we lived there, we had to put up with a boy who was older than us and had been in a reform school. When we were with him, if he went into a store, we stayed back because he would steal anything he could get into his pockets. We were glad to get away from him because we didn't want to be caught with him. We were glad to move away from that apartment.

The only thing I remember about my time in that school was a boy who wanted to wrestle me. I told him that I didn't want to get my clothes dirty wrestling (I didn't have any more), but he kept on telling me I was afraid of him. He kept pushing me until finally I couldn't take any more of his taunting. I threw him to the ground, and the fall broke his arm in three places. He was through wrestling after that. I don't know what happened to him after that, because we moved to West Gastonia and switched schools a few days later. I felt sorry that it happened, and I hope he got well without permanent damage to his arm.

We moved into a house that formerly belonged to the Ozark Cotton Mill, which had been shut down because of the Depression. There was one other house close by. I liked it there and liked the neighbors who lived in the other house. Their family consisted of a seventeen year old boy, a sixteen year old girl, twin girls who were my age, and a baby girl. I liked them because they were poor like us, and we got along well. Also, I was doing well in school, which was only a short walk away, and I liked my teacher.

One boy in my class that year got the best grades on every test, so we thought he was a genius. One day, however, he must have lost sight of the teacher, and she caught him cheating. He never had the best grades again after that. I felt sorry for him and wondered if he ever tried cheating again. You can't get along in this world trying to cheat. The Bible teaches that you can't do wrong and get by with it, "for your sins will always find you out."

There were thirty-eight textile mills operating around Gastonia before the Depression, and most of them were shut down by that year. Jobs were hard to find, but our dad found work at one of the mills that made thread. He worked second shift, and my brother and I took his supper to him at the mill where he worked. We could crawl under the fence to get into the mill. After seeing how people worked there, I never wanted to work in a textile mill. The pay was $12 per week. Our rent was $4 per week, so we lived on the remaining $8.

Most of the mills that were still running had a baseball team in the industrial league. One of the teams played in a park close to where we lived, and when we wanted to watch them play, we could retrieve a baseball hit outside the fence, and they would let us into the game in return for the ball.

Also, we could keep a ball hit outside the park if we needed a ball to play with. We played baseball when we could gather enough boys together to play.

One of the men who lived close by made radios. They were called crystal sets, and he would hang a speaker outside his house and invite us to listen to radio programs. One thing that drew a crowd was the prize fights, especially when Joe Louis was boxing for the championship. The people across the street were not so generous. They owned a radio but never let anyone listen to it. We thought they were rich because the man had a job, and they had a radio.

One of the men who lived above us had an old truck, and he hauled slabs from the saw mill to sell as firewood. To saw them into stove sized wood, he jacked up the rear wheel of his truck and put a belt on it to drive a saw. He then sold the wood for two dollars a load. I don't think he got rich, but he did survive.

Charles and I spent the summer roaming around, looking for scrap metal that we could sell for a little money. One day while we were hunting scrap metal, one of us was poking around in a trash dump. We pulled out an old towel and opened it, and inside there were two dead babies that were about seven or eight inches long. We went to the store nearby and told the people what we had found, and it wasn't long before a crowd gathered. One of the people mentioned that there was a doctor's office close by. I don't know what happened after that, because Charles and I left and continued scrap hunting.

Charles and I, along with a couple of friends, found plenty of things to keep us occupied. Another thing we did in the warm weather was make a swimming pond; it didn't matter to us that the water was always muddy. And, when we heard of someone who was being tried for murder, we went to the courthouse and watched the trial. One such trial that drew a lot of interest was the trial of a person who was killed when he was collecting rent. I don't know how it ended, but we saw most of it. Several murder trials were held in town while we lived there.

All was not play, though. There was a preacher who had Sunday school in one of the empty houses, and I, along with several other young people, attended. I really liked to go hear lessons from the Bible. We were encouraged to learn verses and recite them, and we were rewarded with little gifts when we had memorized them. When the verses were extra long, we got a small Bible as a gift. Almost every night there was a prayer meeting in someone's home in those days. I would go to some of them and join in the singing.

While we were living in the Ozark Mill Community, two women came into the Ozarks and put up a tent right above where we lived, and they held a revival meeting. One of them was a preacher, and the other one led the singing. The preacher said she was a healer, and people would come from miles away to hear her preach. I went every night to join the singing. I though the preacher was the prettiest woman in the world. I believe she was twenty-four years old at the time.

Before she preached, she would take up an offering. She said that she had a bungalow in Dallas, North Carolina, and she needed money to pay for it. She would pass the hat until she got the amount she asked for. I remember her asking for five hundred dollars one time, and she got it while the singing was going on. The singer was twenty-six years old and almost as pretty as the preacher. And, she could really sing.

When Sunday came around, the tent was full of people from several states. Many of them brought someone to be healed. Another boy and I would go to the tent before the meeting started, and when the tent was full, we would sell our seats for a quarter each. We needed the money more than the preacher did.

Some people who lived nearby us had a sick-bed bound lady in their home. Those people had the preacher come to their house to heal the sick woman. I think she was told it would take a while before the healing took effect. This was in the mid 1930s. I don't want to pass judgment on this healing preacher, but after WWII I saw in the newspaper where a woman preacher who lived in Dallas, North Carolina, and had the same name had taken another woman's husband. I don't know if she healed him or not.

My Later School Years

Times being what they were, we did anything legal to make a few cents. During the summer months, there were several men who had trucks loaded with produce, and they hired young men to ride the trucks and go to houses and try to sell their watermelons, cantaloupes, tomatoes, corn, and any other things they had to sell. The boys were paid seventy cents a day. There was a lot of competition among us boys to get this job, and you were lucky to get picked.

Another thing we did was to sell bottles to a man who was a bootlegger. We found empty wine bottles in a part of town called "Greasy Corner" and sold them for a nickel each. (I don't know how that section of town got its name.) We didn't think that was wrong since we weren't actually selling liquor. We did anything we could think of that was honest to make a few cents.

One time when we were attending court as spectators, a well dressed man came up to us and asked us if we would dig him some worms so he could have them to take fishing the next day. We were tickled to do so, and we dug enough for a full can. He gave us fifty cents for the worms.

We also dug worms for ourselves and fished in the Catawba River for catfish with them. Sometimes the bait we used was made with a mixture of cotton and flour dough. Catfish will bite almost anything.

One time when Dad, Charles, and I went fishing, we only had a few worms, so we cut up the first fish we caught and used it for bait. After we had fished all day, we took our catch home, and I counted ninety-seven catfish in our catch. Each one of them was about nine inches long. It took a long time to fix enough of them to feed six hungry people, but the time was well spent when we ate them.

There were several fish camps around Gastonia, and I don't know where the fish they used came from, but they wouldn't want to fool with the nine-inch fish we caught. They always had big fish to eat.

Another thing I did that summer was pick cotton. One of the farmers who grew cotton was hiring people to pick it, and I was looking to make a lot of money if he would hire me. When I asked for a job the farmer looked at me and said, "Son, do you really want to try your hand at picking cotton?"

I answered, "Sir, I sure could use the money to help me when school starts again."

The man looked at me and said, "It sure is good to see someone your age who is willing to work. I'll let you try your hand at it, and I will pay you the same pay as the other pickers — two cents per pound."

I thanked him, and he said, "Come early, and I'll give you a sack to put the cotton in, and when you fill that one, I'll get you another."

I had heard of others picking as much as three hundred pounds a day, and I could see myself being rich when the day was done. Well, I was pretty disappointed because the only thing I had much of was pain in my back. But, I made fifty-four cents that day, which was more than I had the day before. I also learned that I didn't want to pick cotton for a living. That ended my cotton picking. I was also happy, though, because I could use the money I earned to help buy my school supplies when school started again.

Summer ended that year, and I returned to school in the 7th grade. By that time, I had gotten into the habit of putting a bit of chewing tobacco in my mouth. One day the girl sitting in front of me saw me chewing, and she wanted to try it. She wanted to know what I did with the juice, and I told her that I swallowed it and that it didn't make me sick.

I shouldn't have done it, but I gave her some chewing tobacco. It wasn't long before she got sick and asked to go to the restroom. When the teacher asked her what was wrong, I slipped as low in my seat as I could, because she told the teacher where she got the tobacco. I got off with only a lecture about the evils of tobacco, but I felt smaller and smaller as every eye in the room was watching me. I never did that again.

Also, that year, there was a boy who was always in trouble. One day, he had to go to the principal's office for a whipping, but it might not have been such a good idea to whip the boy that day. After the principal removed his belt for the whipping, the boy got hold of the man's pants and pulled them down around his ankles and ran out of the school. Once the principal got his pants up, he ran after the boy and finally pulled him out from under a house. I never heard what they did with the boy, but the principal wore suspenders along with the belt after that.

Across the street from the schoolhouse, there was a large open field where most of the boys went and played ball at recess time. We played with a ball that belonged to the school, and we had to check it in after the bell rang telling us that recess was over. One day, it was my time to turn in the ball, and a rich boy (he had a bicycle) told me to give him the ball. When I didn't let him have it, he started trying to take it from me. When the fight was over, I had the ball and turned it in.

Later on, when school was out for the summer, I was picking blackberries when I looked up and saw the rich boy and his father. His father had a gun, and I thought he was going to shoot me. He didn't shoot me, but he used some strong language, telling me to get off his land and never come back. I was scared stiff and was happy to get away. I never went near their place again.

I did go berry picking again, but this time, I had someone with me. Smidge, the girl who lived next door, wanted to go blackberry picking, and I was glad to have someone to go with me. We started very early, when the dew was still on the grass. We came upon a barbed wire fence, and we saw a lot of berries on the other side. Smidge wanted to go under the fence, and I held the wires apart while she went under, and I got through while she held the wires apart for me.

We found the most and prettiest berries I had ever seen. We started to pick some of them, and someone yelled for us to get out of his berries. We found out why they were so big and pretty — they were his tame berries. We had never seen any domesticated berries before.

We were trying to cross the fence to get out, and when I got hold of the wire to hold it apart, I got shocked. It didn't take me a long time to turn it loose. We had to lie down in the wet grass and crawl under, trying not touch the wire. The man had turned on the power to the fence when he saw us going across it. I learned two things that morning: the berries were tame, and the fence was electric. I couldn't go anywhere around there to pick berries without getting into trouble. It wasn't like back in Canton. I don't think I went berry-picking any more that summer.

We moved again while I was still in seventh grade, but it was not far from school. I finished the school year, and then we moved back to Canton, North Carolina.

Canton Once More

The old farmhouse we moved into in the Thickety community near Canton was about two and a half miles from town. When we went into town, we had to walk barefooted on an old gravel road. We didn't have any shoes. Our feet got hardened after a few trips, and we got used to walking. Sometimes someone would give us a ride, but automobiles were scarce. Sometimes we would walk all the way into town and not see a car. The Depression was hard on everyone, and most families didn't own a car. I liked that house better than anywhere we had ever lived. There was a good-sized creek close by where we could make a pond, and this is where we took our baths during the summer.

We didn't do all of our swimming in the creek. We also went to the Pigeon River to swim. The water in the river was black from the effluent that the paper mill poured into it. It had tannic acid in it, and the rocks in the river were slick. We had a good time sliding down the rocks. The acid in the water was a good healing agent, too. It healed all our sores and cuts. If your dog had the mange, you could throw him in, and it would heal him. You had to throw him in three times, we thought.

The creek that ran from Thickety was called Murray Branch, and we always washed in its clear water after being in the river before going home. We had a lot of good times playing in that old black water. One time when the preacher from the church where the Reed family attended came to visit, he brought his son along. We took the preacher's son to the river for a dip. We missed that old black river when we moved away, and we really liked living in that old house.

When we next moved into the old Willis place, the Oak Grove Baptist Church was being built, and the church members were helping with anything they could do. There were some trees that had to be moved, and they gave us the wood out of a great big oak tree — but we had to dig it up.

The job of digging went to Charles and me. We dug a trench around the tree deep enough to hide inside. One day when we were digging, our dad came up after he got off work to see how we were getting along, and he said he was going to get "Dink" Wines to bring some dynamite to put under the roots and blast the tree out (like the stumps at Beaverdam school). While he was gone, a car drove up and parked across the road, and two men and two women got out of the car and went into the woods. They couldn't see us down in the trench where we were digging.

When Dink and Dad came back, they asked whose car that was. We told them what had happened, and Dink said, "Let's have some fun!"

He took a stick of dynamite and cut it in half. He gave Dad half and put fuses in both halves. Dink took his half and put it on a big old flat rock beside the road and lit the fuse and got out of the way. Dad lit the other half and threw it into the woods. In a few seconds, both pieces went off and made a big sound and threw sticks and leaves into the air.

In no time one man and one woman came running out of the woods, and the man called back to his buddy and said "We'll be going down the road, and we'll pick you up!"

It wasn't but a few more seconds until the other two came out and jumped into the car with them — and down the road they went. I doubt if they ever came back there. Dink set off some dynamite under the tree, which was enough to make the tree fall. We have laughed a lot about that day over the years.

While I lived at the Willis house, I started going to Sunday school. Class was held in an old work bus across the road from the church while the church was being finished inside. Hack Clark and Kelly

Carswell were my teachers. I remember them taking us on a fishing trip to Lake James, and we stayed all night. I was poor but happy in those days.

It was summertime when we moved there, and I went blackberry picking on Grassy Top Mountain. I found a lot of pretty berries. I had my bucket almost full one day when I heard something that sounded like a rattlesnake. I guess he thought I was getting his berries, and I decided that if he wanted me to get out, I would make him happy and leave. I didn't go up there anymore that summer.

Times were hard back during the Depression. We canned all of the food that we could. The first refrigerator I can remember was owned by the Reed family who lived across the road from us. I remember that the brand name was "Frigidaire", and for a long time, everyone who had a refrigerator called it a Frigidaire, no matter who made theirs.

We never had a refrigerator while we were growing up. When we lived in Gastonia, there was a truck that hauled ice, and those who had an ice box could buy ice and keep things cold until the ice melted. We children would wait on the ice man, and he would chip us off a piece of ice to eat.

We never had any electric appliances until after WWII, and then we had to sign up and wait to get anything electrical — a refrigerator, a washing machine, even an electric iron, and also an automobile. Lots of people didn't have electricity in their houses, and later on, when I got my electrical contractor's license, I wired several houses for people. Times are better now than ever before, but I think the younger generation doesn't have as much fun as we had back then.

In those days, you could get all the chestnuts you could carry. We would take a sack and get as many as we wanted. Later, there was a blight that killed all of the trees, and by the time I got out of school, my friend, Tom Jimison, and I went chestnut hunting up on Grassy Top Mountain, and we found, only a hand-full of chestnuts. I think the Agriculture Department is working to get a tree that will withstand the blight and is similar to the one that used to be healthy. We also used to have a small nut called a chinquapin that tasted like a chestnut. We used to gather them and string them up into a necklace, and then bite them off. They are gone now, too. A lot of the old things have disappeared.

There were several apple trees nearby where we lived, which was a first for us. There were also lots of woods close by, giving us plenty of places to hunt squirrels and other game. In the fall and winter months, we hunted opossum and sold their hides to a place in Wisconsin. I learned something about hunting dogs: if they chased rabbits at night, they didn't make good 'possum hunters. Also, if they got sprayed from a skunk, you might as well go back home; they were good for nothing that night.

Some folks ate 'possum meat, but we never did. We rented the house from one of the people who did eat it. He found out that we hunted a lot, and he asked our dad if he would cook him one. My dad told him we were going hunting that Saturday, and if we got a good one, he would cook it on Sunday. Lucky for us, we caught two big 'possums that day. We skinned and dressed them, and when breakfast was over, Dad started cooking them. After parboiling them, he them got ready for baking. In the meantime, my mother fussed at him for using her pots and pans for cooking 'possum. He went ahead anyhow and used salt, black pepper, and red pepper, and cooked them along with sweet potatoes.

The 'possums were finally done roasting about two o'clock, and Dad took them out of the oven. The elderly gentleman had waited patiently and was ready to eat. And, he really did eat. I had been watching, and I decided to try a bite. The meat tasted good, but I couldn't swallow it for looking at the 'possum's nose and tail.

I don't know where we got it, but we had a dog that was good for treeing 'possums. One of my friends who hunted with us wanted to buy it. My dad finally sold it to him on the Sunday after a Saturday night hunt, and the boy who bought him said it never treed another 'possum because he bought it on Sunday.

Hog killing time was one thing that brought several of the men and boys together. I always helped with hog killing whenever I could. There was a place next to the creek where the men had built a place to butcher their hogs. There was a big vat that held five or six hundred gallons of water. On the evening before the slaughter, the men and boys filled the vat with water from the creek, and the next morning, about four o'clock, someone started a fire under the vat.

When the water got scalding hot, the men would kill a hog and bring it to the vat. They would dip it into the scalding hot water until the hair would get loose enough to be pulled out, and then they would take the hog out, lay it on a big table, and scrape the hair off with a big metal scraper. Next, they would hang it from a pole that had been put across the top of some upright poles. There was a sort of assembly line the men used when helping each other until everyone had his hog ready for the women to start cutting the hogs into meat ready for the smokehouse, where it was salted.

In the smokehouse, the meat was either hanged or laid on a big table for curing. The hams and shoulders were hung up to cure. The women trimmed off what they wanted to use to make sausage and carved off some backbone and ribs, which made good eating. They also made liver mush and souse meat. There was a way to eat about every part of the hog, and using every bit of the hog sure was a big help for the grocery bill during the Depression years. We put pieces of pork into canning jars, and we used hog grease to seal them by turning the jars upside down. Nothing was wasted.

After I was married, several years later, I raised a little pig. It was a small variety — I don't know what kind it was. I slaughtered it by myself, and I got about sixty pounds of meat out of it. I kept track of how much it cost to raise the pig, and I learned that I could have bought that much meat for about half of what it cost me to raise the animal. I stopped raising pigs at that point.

Carroll Clark and his wife, Jessie, lived across the road from us. They were really good neighbors. They had a young daughter, Maxine, and a young baby boy named Neil. Carroll had an old white mule named Bert. Bert was a good worker, but you had to catch him first. He was afraid of sudden noises, and when he got scared, he was hard to catch.

One day, I had been working old Bert, plowing in the middle of the corn that we had planted behind the Methodist church, and when we got done (Charles and Dad were working also) it was my time to ride the mule back home. Everything was going well until some of the older boys who had an old T-model Ford came along and (knowing of Bert's problem with a sudden noise) made their old car backfire. Bert didn't take kindly to the noise, and he jumped several feet and wanted to run. Thankfully, I was able to stop him from running away. Once, he ran away with another man and didn't stop until he got too tired to run any more.

I remember one time, Carroll, his brother Charles, my brother Charles, and I ran after Bert all morning trying to catch him before we finally got him to go back into the pasture. When we went into the pasture to catch him, we had to show him an ear of corn or something white, and if we didn't catch him quickly, he would run. But, when we had him in the field working, he was easy to manage.

After summer, it was time for me to start eighth grade, and I didn't have any shoes. When Jessie Clark found out, she gave me a dollar to buy myself a pair of tennis shoes and let me work to pay it back. I walked to school barefoot and was thankful to get shoes. I have never forgotten her for helping me.

Carroll got a job in the paper mill, and one day he started to fall. As he tried to catch himself, he caught hold of a high voltage wire and was electrocuted. His young son, who never could remember his father, is now my Sunday school teacher.

I had a hard time getting started in the eighth grade, but by the next year I had worked wherever I could and had earned enough money to buy some good shoes. All of this couldn't have happened anywhere else.

Another time when I needed school books, another neighbor gave me the books that her daughter had used the year before. Oh, and I ended up marrying that girl a few years later.

I told my dad at that point that if he moved to where I couldn't finish high school, I was not going with him, and I would find someone to keep me. (I don't know if I could have.) My clothes were skimpy, but the Lord kept me from freezing that winter. During the fall and spring months, I picked creasy greens on Saturday and took a sack full with me on the school bus. I would get off the school bus at the company store, where I sold those greens for five cents per pound. I did well enough to pay my way through school.

There was a barn across from the house, and we got a milk cow. It was my job to milk every morning before breakfast, and I still had to catch the school bus at 7:00 AM. I was big enough to carry the milk to the house by this time.

That summer, Charles and I got a job cutting wood for a man. He ran a steel cable up the mountain, and we would staple a stick of wood to the cable and send it down the mountain, where it came off. We earned thirty dollars doing that, but we never got a cent for our work. Our dad kept it all.

Well, we did move again, but only about half a mile to the other side of the hill and woods. For the next two years, I walked back through the woods so that I didn't have to change schools. During school days I wouldn't go 'possum hunting until I got my homework done. I intended to finish high school.

I had a hard time going to school, but school gave me an opportunity that I otherwise would not have had. I took a vocational course that covered woodworking, welding, sheet metal work, and machine work. I chose machine work in order to become a machinist.

During the summer of 1940, there were two floods that hit the community two weeks apart. They did a lot of damage to the town and the local paper mill. The football field was covered with sand, and I got work with a national jobs program to remove that sand, as well as other odd jobs. I was really glad to have the summer job.

The summer of 1941 was good for me. The National Youth Administration (NYA) gave several local young people jobs. Charles and I got jobs, but we didn't have a way to get to Waynesville, North Carolina, where the jobs were. The job we had was building a school bus garage. We got lucky and bought an old Ford for $45. Three riders — our friend John Jenkins and two girls — helped with the expenses.

One day, we were on our way home from work when a new car suddenly stopped in front of us. In spite of Charles hollering "whoa!" and using what brakes we had, we still ran into that new car. We jumped out to see if we would have to pay our summer's wages to fix the new car. We were really happy when the driver of the car told us to go on our way because there wasn't any damage.

Although I owned part of that car, I never got to drive it because I didn't have a driver's license. I'll admit that I was glad I wasn't driving that day. After driving the old car, we sold it for what we paid for it. The wages from that job came in handy for my last year of high school.

Eleventh grade was as far as high school went in those days, and my last year went well. I was the first one in our family to get a high school diploma.

There was a lot of talk about Hitler and his taking Poland, as well as his running over North Africa and France. There was also a lot of concern about England. People were wondering how long they could survive the bombing that came every day and night.

America had a lend-lease program, and the United States was supplying war material to the English and the Russians. All the while, the factories were calling for all the people they could get to work, so they could make ships and aircraft. One day someone came to our school wanting those of us who were working in shops to sign up to work at a factory after we graduated. Several of us filled out applications to work there. The factory was the Glen L. Martin Aircraft factory, located in Baltimore, Maryland. They built the B-26 medium bomber, and several Navy PBM planes.

All of this manufacturing accelerated after Japan bombed Pearl Harbor and destroyed a lot of our ships that were docked there. The bombing happened on December 7th of that year, and the United States was drawn into World War II.

In the spring of 1942, before my graduation, the mountain above Lake Logan caught on fire, and the school sent several of us to help control the fire. My friend, Bruce Sharp, and I went to help. We didn't fight the fire, but we patrolled a trail where the firemen had created a back-fire. We were to let the firemen know if the fire got across the trail. It was a good job for a good cause. We spent one day and night, and we even were fed with the firemen. The paper mill owned the lake, and they sent a truckload of food for us. We got the fire put out without letting the whole mountain burn.

Those of us who had applied for work at the aircraft factory waited until graduation on May 1, 1942, before reporting to work. I didn't have enough money to pay for my train fare to Maryland, so my best friend in school, Bruce Sharp, loaned me enough so we could go together.

One thing I needed to take with me was a birth certificate. I had written to Gaston County, where I was born, to get one, and when the certificate came in, my middle name on it was different from the one I had used all my life. I had thought my full name was Talmadge Junior Fletcher or "TJ" to my friends and family. Whoever filled out my birth certificate had used my mother's maiden name, Pressley, for my middle name.

I didn't have time to change my birth certificate before I went to Baltimore, and since my name on my application didn't match the name on my birth certificate, they didn't hire me. The lady who ran the place where I was boarding told me I could stay at her place until I got my job. I went to the factory to file another application, and they hired me for the job I wanted, a machinist. I went to work right away with my new name, "TP." I never changed the name on my birth certificate. All my school friends and family still call me TJ.

I was boarding at a home in Essex, Maryland, and I rode a bus to work in Little River. Several of the men from Canton were boarding at a place in Little River, and when they had room for Bruce and me, we moved down with them where we could walk to work. At one time, there were twelve of us from

Canton boarding there. It was on a large farm, and we were fed and treated well.

One day Bruce asked, "Have you ever thought about going into the military?" I said I had thought about it, but preferred the Air Force. I didn't think I wanted to be eye-to-eye with someone that I had to shoot. I preferred to drop bombs where I didn't have to see someone die. He told me that the Navy wanted pilots to fly Navy planes, and he talked me into trying for their pilot training. We went to the recruiting office, where we took a written test and a physical exam. We both were accepted, but we had to have our parents' permission to join.

We quit our jobs and went home to get our papers signed. Bruce got his signed, but my parents wouldn't sign for me. Bruce wouldn't go by himself, so we went back to Baltimore and got jobs with Western Electric Company. After about three months, we were old enough that our parents didn't have to sign for us anymore, and we decided to go home again and join the Marines. When we arrived home, Charles wanted both of us to join the Navy so we could go together. We went to enlist, but Charles was turned down because he failed the eye test, and I decided not to go into the Navy. Later on, I realized how lucky I was that I didn't go, because I stayed seasick for fourteen days when I came home from a trip overseas later on.

About the middle of November, 1942, Charles got a notice from the Draft Board that he was being drafted and that he was to report for duty early on the morning of December 2nd. On the same day, Troy Ford, a friend who lived nearby, got a notice to report on the same day. When Troy's brother-in-law, James Trull, found out that Troy and Charles were being drafted, he found me and asked me if I would want to ask the Draft Board if we could be drafted along with Troy and Charles. I told him it sounded good to me. We were prepared to ask if the Draft Board would take James and me in exchange for two draftees who didn't want to go into the military. We found out where to go, and we went to talk to talk to someone at the Draft Board.

When we got there on a Monday, one of the men said, "What can we do for you boys?" When we told them what we wanted, they all laughed, and said this was the first time someone had asked to be drafted, that most boys asked if they could be deferred. They told us that if that is what we wanted, we needed to go to Doctor Johnson, tell him we wanted a physical exam to go into the military, and if we passed, we could join on Saturday. We went to the Doctor and told him what we wanted, and he was surprised that we were eager to go into the military when others wanted to dodge the draft. We both passed the exam, but our blood samples had to be sent to Raleigh for testing.

I remember James Reed's mother telling me, "They won't take a little skinny boy like you." She packed James a suitcase full of things, but I didn't have anything to take. When he took his physical, he was turned down because he had a bad knee, and he was never called again. However, this little 138 pound boy passed the entrance exam.

When Saturday arrived, James and I, along with Charles and Troy, were at the appointed place, ready to get on the bus for Camp Croft, South Carolina. The man with the roster said, "When I call your name, you can get on the bus."

When all the names had been called, I was left standing there alone. I asked the man why he hadn't called my name, and he told me that the results of my blood test hadn't come back from Raleigh yet, so they couldn't let me go.

I asked, "If the results come in the mail today, can I go down to Camp Croft?"

He said, "If it comes in the eleven o'clock mail, you can go on down to where the others are and check in, but if it is not in the mail, you will have to wait until the next group goes on January 29th." I waited on the mail, but it didn't have my blood test results in it. I found out (too late) that it had been sent to the wrong post office, Candler, North Carolina. There was nothing I could do but wait on January 29th, 1943. I was really disappointed that I had missed the December bus.

DRAFTED

When January came, I finally got my wish to get into the Service. At that time, after being enlisted at Camp Croft, they let you go back home for seven days before final induction. I had spent lots of time at home, and I didn't want to go back. Neither did one of my school friends, Howard, so I had a buddy to talk to. We were put on a bus and sent to Fort Bragg, North Carolina, which was the major induction center where they tested and interviewed us to see where in the military the best fit for us would be.

When Howard and I got to Fort Bragg, we were put in line with all the other recruits and issued our Army clothes and assigned to a barracks. When they got to me, they didn't have a hat or shirt that fit me. They got some clothes that were my size later.

Charles and Troy were still at Fort Bragg at that time, and they gave Howard and me some good advice. They said, "When they call all of the new recruits out the first thing in the morning, they call out a bunch of names; don't answer, because you will be put on KP duty."

They were right — the next names called were for the regular KP duty. I got put on a job in the mail room sending the civilian clothes the recruits had been wearing home. I had the job of addressing packages and taking them to the post office to be sent off. That was the only extra duty I had before I left Fort Bragg.

I was given a test in radio skills and was tested for Morse code in a big room with about forty or fifty others. They gave us a test on a series of dots and dashes, and we had to wait while they checked our grades on a machine. After grading the tests, they said that those whose names they called were to stay behind after the others left. My name was called. I thought we had failed and would have to take the test again. However, we were told that we did well on the test, and we were going to take it again to see if the first test's results were accidental. After we took the test again, it was about three weeks before I found out what training I had been assigned to. My friend Howard wanted to go into the Army Signal Corps, and he got his wish.

I was interviewed by one of the officers, and he asked what branch of the service I preferred. I told him that because I had finished high school, been schooled as a machinist, and had worked in the Glen Martin Aircraft Factory, I was well-suited for the Army Air Corps. (The United States Air Force was not established as a separate branch of the military until after WWII.)

I was finally given some clothes that fit. At six feet tall, I weighed 138 pounds. At first I had been given a second-hand hat and a shirt. After six days of testing and interviews, I was assigned to the airbase in Biloxi, Mississippi, where I was to be tested to see if I would make a good aircraft mechanic. I never had to go through basic training. I guess they were so much in need of gunners and other air crew that they let me skip it.

Biloxi, Mississippi

I spent the next three weeks at Keesler Field testing for different aircraft mechanical tasks. During my time there, I had to do KP duties once a week. We had a 24-hour shift, from 4 o'clock in the morning until 4 o' clock AM the next day. It wasn't hard work for me because I was used to working.

My first day at KP, I got into trouble. I was put on the serving line at lunch, serving pork chops like

I had never seen. It wasn't long until I ran out, so I asked for more. The mess sergeant asked what happened to them, and I answered, "They just ran out."

He said, "How many did you give each one?"

I told him that I gave them all they wanted, and the sergeant told me I was only supposed to give one to each person. I said that nobody told me how much I was to give each one. He said, "You remember that the next time."

I told him I had only been in the Army just a few days. He went back into the kitchen and came back with a pan of something that I had never seen. When the rest of the people asked me what it was, I said I didn't know. They said, "It don't look like pork chops!"

The next time I was put on the serving line, the mess sergeant put me to serving bread. He said, "I'm telling you this time, you are to give each one only one slice each, and when he eats that, you can give him another slice, but only one at a time."

I replied, "You can count on me!"

Everything was going along fine until a little sergeant came by and wanted more than one slice. I told him what the mess sergeant told me to do, and he cursed a little and said he would get all he wanted. I said, "Not from me, you won't!"

Somebody else came by the sergeant and grabbed another slice, and I took it away from him. He finally went away, although I suppose he really used some unheard-of names for me, but I was only following orders. I only had to do KP one more time before I shipped out.

I was qualified to be an aircraft mechanic, and I volunteered for aerial gunnery school, thinking I would come back to Biloxi afterwards.

Laredo, Texas

After about four months in the Army Air Corps, I was sent to Laredo, Texas, to gunnery school. It was winter time, and I was glad to go to a warmer climate. It was a lot warmer. Normally we had to wear a tie any time we were off base, but they let us go without one until 5:00 PM, at which time we had to put it on. It paid to have your tie with you at all times.

When I arrived in Laredo, along with seven other potential gunners, we were assigned to a class instructor, and we started our training right away. We had four hours of instruction in the classroom, and then we were taken to a place where they had machine guns loaded with BB shot. We shot at clay airplanes that ran around a track. We were practicing shooting at moving targets so that we could shoot down German and Japanese airplanes.

In the classroom, we had to dismantle 50-caliber machine guns and had to be familiar enough with them to be able to put them back together blindfolded. I never was too good at it, but I learned to shoot all of the guns. We also shot skeet every day with a 12-gauge shotgun.

We flew on training missions where we shot at aerial targets. On my first flight, I was given a machine gun and assigned to an AT-6 training plane. I had never been close to an airplane of any kind, but I climbed into the open rear seat with my gun. I was to shoot at a big sleeve target that was towed behind another trainer. Four planes shot at the target, one after the other. After we shot all of our ammunition, we landed and went to where the sleeve target had landed. The holes in the target were counted (each one had a different color) to see how many hits each of us had. We needed ten percent to pass. On my first try, I only got twelve hits, but I made up for it later when I got over the excitement of flying. One day, we flew in a B36 bomber, and each of us shot from the different turrets (top, ball, tail, and waist gun). Another day, we went about twenty miles out into the desert where they had all kinds of guns set up for us to shoot at different targets.

One thing we didn't shoot at was rattlesnakes. The GIs who were permanently stationed there would catch them and put them in a cage. When they had enough (I don't know how many "enough" was), they sold them to a cannery in town where they canned them and sold them to restaurants. When I was there, they had about a bushel of snakes, and one of the men said if we would pass the hat (which yielded a few coins), he would get one out. He took a stick and raked one out of the pile and held it to the ground. He took his other bare hand and caught it behind the head. Then he lifted it up and wrapped it around his arm. I wondered if he was a member of a snake handling cult or if he just wasn't afraid of snakes. I have always wondered if he ever got bitten.

When our training was drawing to an end, one of the last things we did was ride around a track at 30 mph and shoot at clay pigeons when they came up on the side of the road. We made eight trips, and each of us shot in turn. I hit 23 out of 25 and tied with one of the others who said he had never shot a gun of any kind before joining the Army.

Laredo, Texas, was on one side of the Rio-Grande River, and Mexico was on the other. We could walk across the bridge that joined the two countries. The first time I went to Mexico, I met a man who had a tray full of rings, and he wanted to sell me one. I asked what the price was, and he said, "twenty dollars", and the whole time, he was shining one that was really pretty. After a while of bargaining, I finally got one for two dollars, and I thought I really got a good deal. The ring wasn't on my sweaty finger too long before the pretty ring started to change to copper. I did a lot of looking after that, but I never bought another ring there.

The only money we were allowed to take into Mexico was two one-dollar bills and silver. If you were caught with anything else, you would be put into jail. Our colonel said they would lock you up and throw away the key. At one time, he had a hard time getting a soldier out of jail after he found where he was.

When we got off the bus that took us to town, we were met by several Mexican boys with shoe shining equipment wanting to shine our shoes for a nickel. Over the bridge into Mexico, they would shine them for two cents and dust them off for a penny.

I learned a lesson during my time there: Never play the games at a carnival. The first payday I got, I wanted to go to town. I got a pass and rode the bus to town. When I got off the bus, I spotted a carnival that had just come to town. I don't know what prompted me to go there, but I did, and I went to a game that I had never seen. It had a big board with holes in it and golf balls that rolled down the board and into the holes which had numbers by them. The numbers were added together, and prizes were given for certain totals. When I left the carnival (not long after I arrived), I only had one dime to pay my bus fare back to camp. I learned my lesson. If anyone I knew was going to the fair or to a carnival, I advised him not to go to that golf ball game and warned him that the operator would out-count you every time.

Finally, we were called out into formation and told that the people whose names were called first were going back to Biloxi, Mississippi, to aircraft mechanics school. Again, my name was not called. I had a little brown book showing that I was qualified for mechanics school, so I called to the sergeant and told him I was supposed to go back. He said to wait a minute, because he had another list. He called the names on that list, which my name was on, and said that we were going to Sioux Falls.

Someone asked, "Where in the world is that?" and the answer was "South Dakota." Someone else said, "What is up there?" and the answer was "Radio School."

I was promoted to the rank of PFC before I was sent on to Sioux Falls. There were 27 of us going. We were taken to the train depot the next day, and all 27 of us were put on the same car. A little bit later, we were on our way to where there was snow on the ground. All of our winter clothes were in our bags, stored away where we couldn't get to them. We stopped in Omaha, Nebraska, and found that our summer clothes were not enough for the winter in that part of the country.

The next day, we arrived in Sioux Falls and saw snow all around. When we got to the base, there was a big sign that read "Welcome to Sioux Falls Army Air Base — Pronounced 'Sue'." They knew that there were a lot of us who had never tried to pronounce the word "Sioux", and they wanted us to know the correct pronunciation. We were glad to get our bags, and as soon as we were assigned to a barracks, we lost no time changing into our winter clothes.

Sioux Falls, North Dakota

We settled into the barracks where we were to live (when not in school) for the next six months. The barracks was heated by a large coal burning heater sitting in the center of the room, and if your bunk was close to it, you were in the warmest spot in the room. Everyone in the entire barracks went to school at the same time, and someone had to stay inside to keep the fire going and guard everyone's things. Before my group came, someone had stolen everything he could get, so we were careful not to leave anything where it could be found easily. However, with all the security measures, somebody still stole my leather flight jacket, and it cost me $15 to get another one.

Some of the boys wanted to go to town, but they couldn't get a pass. Someone who had been on the base awhile solved their problem. If they could have someone send them a money order, they could go to town and get it. Several of them knew someone who had a pass go into town and send them a money order for a few dollars (for a fee).

The Commanding Officer there had been making the men wear a big old metal helmet to town. There had been a lot of complaints about it, and he was removed shortly after I got there. I was glad of it. Everything went along smoothly while I was there.

I was assigned to a schedule of classes to learn how to operate and repair the kinds of radio equipment we would be using and to learn how to copy Morse code. (I must have made a good grade on the test at Fort Bragg.) I was happy to be doing something that was needed for my final destination. They had school in three shifts — first shift was from 10:00 AM until 6:00 PM, second shift was from 6:00 PM until 2:00 AM, and third shift was from 2:00 AM until 10:00 AM (graveyard shift). We had to rotate attending all three shifts while we were in school.

My group started school on the first shift, which consisted mostly of explanations of how to operate and repair the equipment we would be using. We were to learn to take Morse code at the rate of twenty words per minute. It sounded impossible at first because we started at a rate of six words per minute. We had to write the words on paper, and each word consisted of five letters. It wasn't as hard as it sounded, and most of us could copy six words.

We learned all about the BC375 model transmitter that had a tuning unit of several frequencies and the BC348 receiver. The same routine of studying and repairing these units was followed for most of our time until the last couple of weeks.

We also did PT (physical training) every day, which consisted of climbing ropes over walls, swinging over ponds, running, and other physical things. One day when I was trying to swing on the "monkey bars", I couldn't do it, and a lieutenant was watching me. He called me over and said, "I have been watching you, and you are sick." I told him I would be all right, and he said, "I am giving you an order — you go on sick call right now!" He took my name and said, "I'll be checking on you, and you'd better go now." I went, and they put me into the hospital for an infected throat. I was in the hospital for two weeks, and I was given a series of pills to cure my infection.

Another patient was in bed beside me and was watching the nurse administer my pills. He told me when she left that he had been there two weeks, and they couldn't find his problem. He said he had seen almost all of the doctors, and all they gave him was water. He was discharged a few days later. After I was discharged, I went over to his squadron to see him. He was in a poker game, still complaining that something was wrong with him. Everyone just figured he was trying to get out of the Army.

Time was passing rather quickly. After passing six words per minute in school, doing eight and ten words per minute was pretty easy. By the time I got to fourteen words per minute, I thought I would never get past that speed.

I was on the second shift one night, and I went to sleep. The corporal in charge told me to set my chair on the table and take my code standing up. When I asked him to let me go and wash my face in cold water, he wouldn't let me go. After a little while, I went to sleep standing up. About that time, the officer of the day came by and woke me up and asked me why I was standing. I told him I just fell asleep. He said, "Go and wash your face in cold water, and that will help you stay awake." I replied that I had asked the corporal to let me go, and he wouldn't let me. The officer talked pretty rough to the corporal, and told him that if anyone got sleepy, they were to be allowed to go and wash themselves in cold water.

They gave me a code check a little later, and I was the only one who passed fourteen words per minute. After that, I passed sixteen words per minute (the rhythm was easier than fourteen), and the next week I passed eighteen, and a few days later, twenty words per minute. I could copy a few words at twenty-two, but I couldn't write any faster.

We had a boy in our barracks whose name was Burkhalter. He was always doing something funny. The barracks didn't have a ceiling, and he would act like a monkey by swinging on the rafters. One night before he went to school, he was sleeping, and one of the other men painted a big purple mustache on him. He went to school without knowing it was on his face. The next day, he put his bunk up on the rafters and slept there.

Another thing I did while going to radio school was to help my friend. He was married, and his wife came to see him on a night he had school. The only way he could miss school was to be sick. He talked to me, and we came up with a solution: I would go on sick call in his place. I memorized his army serial number, and I went on sick call in his place. I had to think of something to be sick of, and all I could think of was to tell them I had a 100 degree temperature. They almost sent me to the hospital. I told them all I needed was something for constipation. That was the wrong thing to tell them, because I didn't get back to the barracks before I had to stop at the latrine. Then, I had to go three more times before I had to go to school. I had ended up being sick for real. Oh well, anything to help a buddy.

My friend's name was Brown, and he shipped out before I did. He bought a pair of dress shoes that didn't fit him but fit me. He said I could keep them and when he got to where he was going, he would write me and I could send him five dollars. He sure did trust me, and when he let me know where he was, I sent him the money.

About two weeks before we graduated, we flew around in a single engine plane and practiced sending and receiving messages. The summer had been awfully hot, and now that winter was approaching, we were getting snow. In the latter part of November, we had a three-day blizzard. We were about to finish radio school, so it didn't bother us much. We had to exercise in our barracks, and the snow drifted between the barracks and the latrine (bath house).

The week before Christmas, 1943, I was sent to a base where it was a little warmer — I thought. After graduation, I was promoted to sergeant and was sent to Kearns, Utah, (about 30 miles from Salt Lake City). To my surprise, snow was everywhere there, too.

Me in the Army Air Corps

Kearns, Utah

The transfer didn't get me out of cold country, like I was hoping, but it wasn't any colder than where I'd just come from. The reason I was sent to Kearns was to have a refresher course in radio. There were several of us, and the course lasted from three days to three weeks, depending on how quickly we could pass the tests. Those of us who were fresh out of school didn't have any problem passing in three days, but the ones who had been out of radio school for awhile had a harder time getting back into the rhythm of copying twenty words per minute of Morse code.

So, after three days, I was out of school and had nothing to do except wait for my next phase of training. The only time I was off base was New Year's Day that year. Half of us had leave on New Year's Day, and the rest had leave on Christmas. They took us into Salt Lake City.

One day, about two-thirds of the men in our barracks were shipped out, and they left the barracks in a mess. As luck would have it, the officer of the day (OD) came in the back door, and I was the first one he saw. He used some bad words, asking what had caused the mess. I told him most of the men had shipped out and had left the mess. He asked who the Barracks Chief was, and I told him it was the corporal, but, he wasn't there. The OD said, "I am putting you in charge," and he told me that he would be back in 30 minutes and that the barracks needed to be cleaned up, or I would be sorry. I could see my Sergeant rank flying away.

I really got lucky, though, because the corporal came in. The officer asked who he was, and when he told him his name, the officer asked if he was the Barracks Chief. He answered that he was, and the officer gave him the order to clean up instead of me. That officer didn't come back, but he sent another person to inspect the barracks, and the corporal didn't pass inspection. I found out later that he was court-marshaled and busted down to private.

One day while I was there, I was watching a group of men in the barracks playing poker when the first sergeant came in and caught them. He said, "Come with me." When I didn't follow, he said to me, "You too."

I said, "Sergeant, I wasn't playing."

He replied, "That don't matter — you was with them!" He marched us to the orderly room to see the officer of the day and told him, "Sir, I caught these men gambling."

The officer had to do something, so he said, "There is a pile of benches out there in the snow. Take these men out there and have them move the benches inside." After we moved them inside, he said, "Put these men on KP duty tonight." However, all of the others had to go to school that night, and I was the only one (and me innocent) that had to go to KP. He had us report to the orderly room at 8:00 the next morning. When we got there, we had to sweep and mop the floor.

After we got that job done, we were standing out in the cold, and I said, "I am going in there to ask what he wants us to do now."

All of the others said, "Don't do that; we will have to work all day!"

I said, "I am the only innocent one here, and I don't deserve this, but I had rather work than stand around in the cold." When I asked the officer what he wanted us to do, he said, "Go back to your barracks and wait, and if I come, you had better be there." We waited all week, and he never came. I don't think the officer wanted to punish us, but he didn't have a choice since the sergeant arrested us. Everybody called that sergeant "Old Blood and Guts."

Most of the men in the barracks had to go to school, and it was late when they got in bed.

Sometimes, Old Blood and Guts came into the barracks blowing his whistle and turning on the lights. One night, we took all the light bulbs out, and when he came in blowing his whistle, he reached up and pulled the cord and nothing happened. He shined his flashlight and started cursing because all the sockets were empty.

Someone at the far end of the barracks said, "You are crazy!" I won't use the language they used, but the words flew back and forth for a while.

Finally, Old Blood and Guts said, "I'll go get the OD."

Someone from the other end of the barracks said, "Go get him. You're blind and don't know how to turn a light on!"

The sergeant cursed some more and left. We put all the bulbs back in, and when Old Sarge brought the OD back, he said, "Look here, Sir, they took all the bulbs out!"

But when the OD reached up and pulled the cord, the lights came on, and he said, "There is nothing wrong with these lights." The OD said, "You men will hear from me about this!" I think the OD was happy Old Sarge had been taken. We never heard from the OD.

The men who had been caught gambling bought some poker chips, and sure enough, Old Blood and Guts marched them (I stayed away from them) to the OD and said, "I caught them again, Sir! They were gambling again!"

The OD said, "Where is the money?"

Old Sarge said, "They didn't have money; they were playing with chips."

The OD said, "Sergeant, you ought to know better. You can't accuse them for playing with chips!", and he said the men could go.

It was not more than a few days later when Old Sarge was busted down to private. There were no excuses when you were scheduled to go to the firing range, and when the sergeant failed to go, he was demoted to private. He had failed to see his name on the bulletin board. After that, he was called "Private Old Guts."

After I was there two months with nothing to do, and most of the others had shipped out, I wondered why I hadn't been given my next assignment. I wanted to leave, so I went to the shipping section and asked why I hadn't been shipped out yet. They told me that according to their records, I was still in school. When I asked the school, they said that according to their records, I had been shipped. I got out the next day.

Tucson, Arizona

I was glad to get on the bus for Davis-Monthan Air Base in Tucson, Arizona, headed towards warm weather. I was not the only one checking in — there were others from different places as well. There were enough people to make a complete

Our Crew. Standing, L-R: James R. Watson (Copilot), Paul C. Karr (Pilot), George F. Miller (Navigator), Douglas Granzow (Bombardier). Kneeling, L-R: Robert P. Sanchez (Flight Engineer), Leland A. Garlock (Tail Gunner), Floyd F. Jensen (Dispatcher), Talmadge P. Fletcher (Radio Operator). (We had two more Gunners, Fitzpatrick and Lawler, who were later taken off our crew and sent to other bases.)

bomb group, although we found out later that we were a group of replacement crews. After I checked in, I was assigned to a barracks and to a combat crew. Then, after being assigned to my crew, we met with our pilot, Paul C. Karr, who was from Erie, Pennsylvania, along with the rest of our new crew. We began preparing for combat training. I was promoted to Staff Sergeant at this point.

We were going to fly the B-24 heavy bomber, and we flew one almost every day or night for our training. I wondered why we flew so much at night — more than during the day. During our training missions, we dropped bombs with five-pound explosives at targets in the desert and fired our machine guns at ground targets. I didn't do much shooting because I was busy sending and receiving messages on the radio. I was assigned several radio stations to communicate with. The pilots were training in Link Trainers when they were not flying the B-24. The trainers had all the things that were on the regular plane.

There was one time I was to do some firing. The training mission was a long one, and the mess hall fixed us sandwiches. I also got a bottle of milk and an orange. After our high altitude bombing, I ate my orange and drank some milk. I didn't know we were going on to a low altitude gunnery mission where everyone was to fire at ground targets. I made it through the bomb bay and met one of the instructors. He was vomiting into an ammunition box, and I got one end of it. There were twelve of us on the plane, and every one of us got sick except our pilot, Lt Karr. That was the only time I got sick while flying. I never ate another orange and never drank milk while flying after that. We really had a perfumed airplane by the time we landed. I never got to fire at anything that day.

We were off duty most weekends, and we were able to go into town or rest in our barracks. We were told by the other men that the base CO (commanding officer) was really strict about Army discipline, and if he saw a shirt unbuttoned or a shoe untied or anyone without a cap, he would have him demoted to private. (Most everyone was a sergeant.)

One day Jensen and I were going into Tucson. Jensen had a cigar in his mouth and his hand-made shoes that he bought in Mexico in a bag under his right arm when we met the colonel. I was able to salute, but Jensen was trying to remove the cigar and shift his shoes to his other hand so he could salute, and he never made it. He tried to explain, but the colonel told him that he should always be

B-24 "Liberator"

able to salute at any time he met an officer. We both thought that he would have Jensen demoted, but he didn't. He might not have been as mean as we had been told.

We finished our training about the middle of May, and I was promoted to Technical Sergeant. Then we were sent to Lincoln, Nebraska, where we were given a brand new B-24 to fly and check out. It had been tested before, and it had about 10 hours of flying time on it. We flew it for about seven hours. We stayed in Lincoln about six days, before we were sent overseas to England.

WORLD WAR II

 I don't know how many crews in our group were going to England. Some crews flew to Brazil and then to their destination. My crew left Lincoln at midnight, and stopped at Bangor, Maine, for fuel and then again at Goose Bay, Labrador, for more fuel. We ate a meal in Goose Bay, but I don't know which meal it was. We were hungry and ate whatever we were given.

 We left Goose Bay at midnight to fly to the United Kingdom. We flew at a very low altitude over the Atlantic Ocean. When we had been in the air for a few hours, the pilot called the navigator and asked for our position. About thirty minutes later, he called again, and George said his equipment wasn't working. I had been listening and was ready when he called me to see what I could get on the radio. All my training was not in vain, because in about two or three minutes, I had a first-class fix and the direction we were to use to reach our destination. We arrived safely at Nutts Corner, Ireland, about twelve miles from Belfast, and I was fully accepted as a crew member that day.

We were in Nutts Corner two or three days. Some of the officers visited Belfast, but the rest of our crew decided to visit the GI Barber Shop. We all decided to have all of our hair cut off. I was selected to be first, but after they saw me with mine gone, the others backed down. It wasn't too bad — I didn't have to comb my hair for two or three months, and I didn't have to use hair tonic.

Harrington, England

After they arranged for us to leave, we were taken to a boat. After about five hours of sailing across the Irish Sea, we landed in Scotland. We marched to the railroad station in Kettering, and after riding a few miles on a train, we were met by an Army truck, which took us to our base in Harrington, England. We were not the only crew to go to Harrington. We found there were four more crews from Tucson there.

When we all unloaded, we were taken to a large room and welcomed to the base. We then were told that if we decided to stay with the group, we would be flying at night and at extremely low altitudes over enemy territory. That was all they would tell us at that time. We were told that if any one wished to leave it would not be held against him, and he would be assigned to another group. No one got up to leave. Then, we were told that we would be a part of a highly secret group that was being formed as the air arm of the Office of Strategic Services (OSS) led by William Donovan. (After World War II, the OSS became the CIA.)

We would be taking arms and supplies to a resistance group, the Free French Underground "Maquis", in enemy occupied territory, where what we took them would be used to sabotage the enemy by destroying railroads, communications, and anything that would slow them down. In addition, we would be carrying secret agents, who would be dropped by parachute. The agents were called "Joes." Some of the Joes included Bill Donovan and Bill Casey, who were heads of the operation.

Our B-24s were painted black, and the ball turret and waist guns and nose turret were removed. The hole that was left after the ball turret was taken out was called "the Joe hole", since that was where the Joes jumped to the ground from an altitude of 600 feet. It was also the hole through which most of the supplies and ammunition were dropped by parachutes from an altitude of 400 feet.

The agents would meet with resistance groups and find where the supplies were needed most and where the targets were to be. The targets were in clearings wherever our loads could be dropped without being seen. Sometimes the Germans found out about the target, and in that case we didn't drop our load. We had a secret signal that was given from the ground, and if we didn't get the proper code we didn't drop, but took the load back to England. Our operation's secret code name was "Operation Carpetbagger", and we came to be called "the Carpetbaggers." (Information about the Carpetbaggers can be found at www.carpetbaggers.org and at the Carpetbagger Aviation Museum in Harrington, England.)

The enlisted men were assigned to our hut on the 5th day of June, 1944, one day before D-day. None of the men would talk about what they were doing because everyone was sworn to secrecy. The ones who had gone on a mission that night would talk to each other and were talking about all the fireworks they had seen on the shores of France, and we found out about the invasion.

Three of the crews that were with us in training and joined us at Harrington were assigned to the same hut. We had to do a lot more training before we were sent on missions, and we were not told much. When they found out that we were not spies they started talking.

There was a pub in a small village about two miles from Harrington, and several of the airmen went there for a pint and a game of darts. I think there is a dart board in every pub in the United Kingdom. We had one in our hut, and those of us who played were good players, often out-playing the English players in the pubs.

We were told a story of another squadron that was in Harrington before we arrived. One night, they waited for the chance, and they stole a barrel of beer, rolling it about two miles back to their squadron. They had a beer party, so it didn't take long for the thieves to be found, and they had to pay for the beer. I suppose they had a hard time rolling the barrel that far and also had a hard time paying for it.

One day while I was playing checkers with one of the other crewmembers (Howe), the commanding officer of the group came into the hut and someone called us to attention. I was where I couldn't see him, and he asked where Fletcher was. Someone told him where I was, and he came around to where I was sitting.

When I started to get up, he said, "Keep your seat." I wondered why he was looking for me.

He asked if I wanted to go on a mission that night, and I answered, "Yes Sir."

He said, "Go up to the squadron office and get with Crance. He will be your pilot, and he will tell you what to do."

I met with the lieutenant at the operations office and told him who I was and that I would be his radio operator. I told him that the CO had sent me, and I asked him what I needed to do, as it was my first mission. He had already been told I was coming, and he welcomed me to my first mission and told me what I needed to do.

I went to the radio office where they gave me a code book and the colors of the day. We had a flare gun and two cartridges with the colors of the day — one for before midnight and one for after midnight. They were to be fired in case of emergencies. I received details of all the radio stations I might have to call in case of emergency, all the transmitter frequencies, and everything else I might need. I also had the secret code, which the resistance group was to give us when they were ready for our drop of arms and other supplies they needed to fight the Germans. We went out to the plane we would be flying later that night and spent all afternoon tuning the radios to the proper frequencies we might need for the mission.

After I had everything ready for any emergency I could think of, I went back to the hut to wait. The take off time was 10 o'clock PM, and I was ready to go. I got my flight suit and my parachute, and I was about the first one to arrive at the airplane. After the crew arrived, we took off on time and flew at a low altitude so it would be hard for radar to pick us up. We had a safe trip to the target area, where we got the secret code. We then dropped our load of supplies and headed back to Harrington. We didn't take any Joes that night, but we had a successful mission and came home safely. I had my first combat mission on July 3rd and 4th. (The mission took a part of two days.) Our crew, led by Lt Karr, flew its first combat mission on July 16th, the first of 30 missions.

801st/492nd Bomb Group

After our training we started missions as a crew. Things were a lot different from what they had been in the USA. One thing that was different was taking a bath. We didn't have much hot water, and we only had one hot bath a week. We had to be tough to take a bath in cold water, or else take a sponge bath in hot water. Everyone in my hut was pretty clean, and all of us smelled about the same except Shorty. He heated water in his helmet on our little stove to shave (he had to shave), but no one ever saw him at the weekly bath.

We didn't get a three-day pass each month (as was usually given), but we were given a four day furlough with the understanding that on the last day we were to be back at noon so we could go on a mission that night. However, the radio operator on Hassart's crew didn't come back at noon once because he said his papers said the leave was not over until midnight.

Later, when he read the bulletin board, he saw a notice for him to report to the orderly room. He came back and said they had his rank wrong. He said, "I am a technical sergeant, and the notice says 'private'." When he checked in with the First Sergeant, he was told that since he was not back by noon, someone else had to go on a mission in his place. He never came back late again.

We normally could go off base, but we had to be back by five o' clock. When Sanchez and I were in town, our captain, "Archie", arranged to call us at the USO club if we had a mission. One time it happened, and he called us back to go on a mission. Captain Archie was a good officer.

One time, Jensen, our dispatcher, had to be back, and he was trying to catch a ride. A big lorry (truck) was going slow, and when it didn't stop and pick him up, Jensen jumped on the back of it. When it got to where he needed to get off, it was going pretty fast, and Jensen beat on the top of the cab. The truck didn't stop, but Jensen jumped off anyway. He was bruised and skinned all over, but he made it back for the mission that night. He was sore for a few days afterwards.

After we came back from a mission, we had to go to a de-briefing to tell how the mission went and give all of the details. The flight surgeon gave each one of us a shot of whiskey to calm us down. Nobody on our crew drank, and I would take all the whiskey to the cook. The only time we had fresh eggs was after a mission, when we got two. But, when I gave our whiskey to the cook, our crew got all of the eggs we wanted.

One time, Sanchez and I were in London just looking around, and we decided to go see Madam Tussaud's Wax Museum. As we entered, we saw a man with a box who was taking up tickets, but he turned out to be a wax figure. He looked so real, I accused Sanchez of speaking to him. I bet a lot of people actually did speak to him. The talent used to create life-size figures of historical persons out of wax is a wonder. We saw wax figures of all the presidents and a lot of the prominent people of world history. The museum also displayed various means of torture that had been used to punish people or put them to death. It was quite interesting to see all of the primitive ways of torture. Beside the guillotine was a wax figure of a man with his hand cut off with blood on it that looked real.

After walking around some more, we decided to hunt a good place to eat. We were told there was a place where Robin Hood used to eat. I don't know if they really did believe it was true or not, but we decided to try it. We got a good meal, but if we had known what it was going to cost, we would not have gone. Our meal cost eight pounds, which was about thirty-eight US Dollars. We never went there again.

After we got tired, we went to a home where an elderly lady kept us. She treated us as if we were her children. When we had used up our time, we caught a train back to Northampton, bought some fish and chips, and rode a bus back to our base. All of the people in England treated us like family.

One time when Sanchez and I were on leave

and were supposed to catch the train to London, we missed the train and had to catch one several hours later. When we got to London, we were looking for the Little Angel Hotel that we always went to, and instead we found a big hole in the ground. We thought we were in the wrong place, but when then we found a bobby (policeman), and asked what happened, he said that a V-2 rocket hit the hotel during the night and destroyed it. We realized that the rocket had hit about the time we would have been there if we had not missed our train. We sure were lucky to miss the train.

Our crew continued flying missions without being shot down. We were luckier than some others. One crew that came in after my crew got shot down on their seventh mission. I believe the good Lord looked after us because we had a good moral crew.

Carpetbagger Monument and Pilot Paul Karr

One night we flew to Denmark, and when we went to the drop site, we were given the wrong signal, so we headed back home with the load. We lost one of our engines because of a drop in oil pressure. We flew over an air base, and they sent up a flare. We didn't know if it was meant for us or the German ME109 fighter that went by. We didn't shoot at him and hoped he didn't shoot at us. He didn't, and we spent about five hours over the North Sea with three engines. One of the other engines had an erratic oil pressure, but it lasted until we got back to the English coast. I called the emergency station, and they told us to land at the closest base, which we did, and they sent another crew to pick us up.

While we waited to be picked up, the enlisted men were told to go to the sergeant's mess hall. We had a cup of tea and a piece of toast and a spoonful of powdered eggs. We were lucky that night. They only had 500 gallons of 100 octane gas, and it was pumped into our tank. When we got ready to take off, we had a lot of spectators come out to watch us take off from the short runway, and we took off with room to spare. We were blessed with two good pilots.

We had engine trouble another time while coming back from our mission, and we landed at a Navy base and ate breakfast with their crew. They had a good meal. That time, they sent an Army vehicle after us and had mechanics to repair the airplane and bring it back.

We had strict orders to not let anyone take pictures of our plane or the crew. One time we landed at another base because we didn't get the proper code signal. We had two Joes with us, and our dispatcher, Jensen, was guarding the plane. Under no circumstance was he to let anyone near the plane or take pictures of it. While he was standing guard, a lieutenant came out with his camera, and Jensen told him not to take a picture of our plane. The officer cursed Jensen and told him he couldn't keep him from taking pictures. Jensen said, "I've got orders, and if you take a picture of that plane, I'll shoot you." Jensen had his 45 pistol out, and the officer cursed some more, but he didn't take a picture, and we wouldn't let anyone near the plane.

Our co-pilot, Watson, called our base, and they sent a vehicle to pick up the Joes. It backed up to the bomb bay and got the Joes without anyone seeing them, and they sent another plane for the crew. It was really important that our plane was not found with all the changes that had been made to it. It was highly secret, and we had orders not to talk about what we were doing.

When the invasion of southern France was taking place, our crew, along with five others, was chosen to take ten paratroopers each and drop them a few miles behind the German army. There, they were to destroy communications and do anything else that would slow down the German army. Along with the paratroopers, we also dropped our usual load of twelve containers to the Maquis, and they used what we dropped to do their sabotage missions.

That was our longest mission. It was over twelve hours long, and it was daylight when we got back to Harrington. I have often wondered how many of the paratroopers had survived their dangerous mission. They contributed a lot to our winning the war.

Belgium and France: Gas Haul

After the Germans were run out of France, General Patton's army was moving so fast that their gasoline supplies couldn't keep up with them. Their gasoline was running low, and we were called upon to fly gasoline to them. The airplanes we used were modified so we could haul 80 octane gasoline. (Aircraft used 100 octane.) My crew was chosen to be one of the crews to haul gasoline.

Our first trip was to a base in Belgium that the Germans had been run out of a few days before. It was late in the day when we landed, and it was an all night wait until our plane was unloaded and we could go back to Harrington. Sanchez and I went into the little village that was close by, and one of the MPs told us that there were snipers still around, and that we should go back to our plane. We went back, and I went up in the operations tower and stayed all night. I could hear all the calls as airplanes came back from their missions.

One call came in from a plane and said, "My radar is out, and I want you to call off the anti-aircraft guns that are shooting at me." Another call was from a fighter plane that couldn't get one wheel of his landing gear to come down and asked to have the firemen stand by. I watched as the P-61 night fighter came down on one wheel. He went as long as he could on one wheel, went down on one side, and slid down the runway with sparks flying, but the airplane didn't catch fire.

When the gasoline was unloaded, we were glad to go home. We got back in time to eat breakfast, and we were tired, sleepy, and ready to "hit the sack." We hadn't been in bed more than an hour when we were called to make another haul. This time we were sent to Lille, France. The unloading crew there had better pumps for unloading, and we were on our way home in less time than before. This time we got to sleep all night before another trip.

Once while we were in France, we had time to explore our surroundings. We were flying with a short crew — we had two pilots, a navigator, a flight engineer, and me. One of the crew had to guard the plane, and four of us went exploring. We spotted what we thought was some kind of store, and when we opened the door and went inside, we found that there were people living there. We apologized for our intrusion. Watson tried to talk in French, and after he stammered a while, a lady spoke up and said in perfect English, "I lived in Chicago for twelve years." This was the only place they could find to live in. We didn't see anything else to explore, so we went back to the airplane. It was soon unloaded, and we went back to our base.

One other time we had to stay all night in France, and Lt Watson and I went into town. We rode in a truck going to town, and when we started to walk back, it was dark except for the moon. We were looking for the road back when we saw a man walking toward us. He had something in his hand that looked like one of the old pine knots I used to gather for kindling. When we met, all he wanted to do was to kiss us on both cheeks. We let him, and he showed us the road to take. He was happy that the German troops had been run out of France. By the time the gasoline hauling was over, we had made seven trips. Our group hauled a total of 822,791 gallons of 80 octane gas to Patton's army.

Spetchley Park, Worcester, England

After we were through hauling gasoline to General Patton, we didn't have anything to do. The CO decided that we were tired and should have some rest, and we were given a week's vacation at Spetchley Park, near Worcester, England. I don't know what the house was used for before the war, but it was being used for a good cause during the war. It was a place large enough to take care of fifty of us at a time.

My crew was the only one from Harrington, but there were enough people from other groups to make a full house. That particular week, they only had forty-nine of us because a man named Garlock got off the train at Birmingham and didn't show up. We found out later that he was demoted and fined most of his pay. No wonder he always wanted to borrow money.

Those staying at Spetchley Park consisted of enlisted men only. The officers went to another place. We had another man who was assigned to our crew who was the operator of a new radar machine, so our crew of five were staying at the rest and recreation (R&R) site. Another man, Keesey, hadn't been on a mission, but he got to go with us.

We were looked after by six USO women during our stay. They gave us civilian clothes to wear, and we could wear them anywhere we went. One of the ladies took us golfing. I went along, although I had never held a golf club before. I enjoyed the outing and watched those who could play. I tried to play golf, but all I could do was lose the ball in the weeds.

The house had a large recreation room with a snooker table. It was larger than the pool table I was used to, and the game took a lot more skill than shooting pool. They had group of local folks to furnish our meals and all the other things it took to keep the house running.

On Saturday they had a dance they called the Virginia Reel. All I could do was watch, since I couldn't dance. One of the ladies, Phyllis, was a palm reader, and I let her read my palm. I got good news because she said I had a long life-line, and she said I would live to be seventy years old. After that I didn't worry about being shot down, and it must have worked. I enjoyed the week of R&R, but I was glad to be going back to Harrington to get in my last two missions and go home.

Back to Harrington, England

One day our colonel was flying one of our planes to the junk yard for airplanes, and he wanted our crew to fly along and bring his crew back to Harrington. He said that the plane wasn't worth repairing. As luck would have it, one of the engines on our plane had trouble and had to be shut down, and it looked like we had junked the wrong plane. We came back OK and made a perfect three-engine landing, and the colonel said that it was the best landing on three engines he had ever seen. I think that our crew were chosen for any extra trips because we were always going somewhere in-between assignments.

One time, they got a new blind landing system. It was installed on three different planes, and my crew was one of the three to test it. One crew didn't get off the ground. One crew took off, but something happened and they had to land without testing the system. We were the only crew that tested it. We took off and landed three times, and it worked. But, I would rather land without it.

France Again

One Sunday, Sanchez and I were in the parachute room (where it was warm) when our operations officer, Captain Archambault, came in and said, "I have been looking for you."
I said, "What have I done now?"
He answered, "Do you want to go to France?"
I told him, "I can't go. I don't have any money."
He gave me ten shillings and said, "Who else would give you money and let you go on a trip like that?"
I asked, "When and where and who with?"
The next morning, I met Lt Abner Pike, who told me to be ready to go after breakfast, and that we were taking a C-47.

The weather was bad all over Europe that winter, and it was pouring rain when we landed at Lyon, France. I knew what our mission was. When someone got shot down and survived or had escaped from a German labor camp and was hidden by the French resistance groups, we would go to France and bring him back to England on one of the trips we made to drop off a load of supplies. The weather got worse, and we didn't go back to England for a few days, hoping for better weather.

I found that a mess hall was a long way from the airfield, and a bus went to it. The bus was slow, and it never stopped — you had to catch it on the run. After one trip, I asked one of the officers where they ate, and he said they ate in the dining room at my hotel. They signed a chit and paid what was the equivalent of 20 cents in English money and got a good meal with a string band playing as they ate.

Lt Pike said, "Go to the hotel restaurant and sign a name you know back at the base and eat there." That is what I did for the rest of our stay. A string band played, and when I wanted more, I said, "Entrée", to the waiters and they brought more. The officers on my crew stayed at a different hotel than I did, so nobody knew me.

One day I was eating, and a major sat down with me and asked what position I held on the plane. I told him that I was the radio operator and that I didn't want to go way out into the country to eat at the mess hall. He said, "I don't blame you; I wouldn't either."

I had a list of several men in the squadron who had given me money to buy them something while I was in France. So, my first day, I shopped for things that they wanted (mostly perfume), and I bought Captain Archie a present with his ten shillings.

We stayed until Saturday, hoping it would stop raining, but it didn't, and our pilot decided to go anyway. We had twenty-one of the men we went after, and they were anxious to go. We flew in the rain at a very low altitude all the way back to Harrington on Christmas Eve, 1944. I gave Captain Archie the present I bought for him, and he called for transportation to take me to my hut. The men we brought back were happy to be alive and back in England, and I was glad to be back from France.

During the week I was gone, the Glenn Miller band, which was entertaining the troops, disappeared while flying across the English Channel. Nobody knows what happened to them.

Winter that year was the worst in a hundred years, and the Battle of the Bulge was taking place.

England: Last Missions

After the gas hauls, we didn't have much to do, except for going to Burtonwood, England, the location of a supply depot, to get supplies and taking other routine flights. Watson, our co-pilot, wanted me to go with him to see his girlfriend in Cambridge. He checked out a plane and got a co-pilot to go with him, and we went to see his friend. I went as both radio operator and flight engineer. It wasn't a long trip, and after we landed (Watson made a perfect landing), I waited in the plane for a couple of hours while he visited his girlfriend. After he visited, we made the trip back to Harrington without any trouble.

We finally started flying missions again. This time we went on bombing missions: We flew diversionary missions for the RAF. We had six five-hundred-pound bombs and six flare bombs that were set to explode at four thousand feet altitude. On our 29th mission, we bombed the factory districts in Dusseldorf Germany. We were shot at by German anti-aircraft guns, but we were not hit.

When we got back to our base, we were at two thousand feet altitude in a landing pattern when Sanchez found one of the flare bombs had hung up in the bomb bay. He called the bombardier, and he and Sanchez disarmed it and got it back in the bomb rack. In the meantime, Watson called the tower and told them what was happening. We were told to go above four thousand feet while air traffic control decided what to do.

The control tower eventually decided it was safe to land, and we went back to two thousand feet, preparing to land. Then the tower called and told us to go to the practice field at Oxford and drop the bomb there. Watson then told them if we did, we would not have enough gas to land, and we would have to bail out and the plane would crash. Watson told them, "We have been low enough to land two times, and nothing happened. If you folks are not afraid the flare bomb will explode when we land, we are not afraid."

They gave us permission to land, and they had firemen and ambulances on standby. Obviously, we landed safely. If the stuck bomb had not been discovered before we landed, I don't know what would have happened that night. The Lord surely must have looked after us.

After the 29th mission, we were scheduled for our 30th and last trip. We went back to the Ruhr valley for another time, and the Germans put their searchlights on us while we were on our bombing run, and we couldn't make any evading moves. The bomb bay doors sometimes drifted shut, and the bombs were dropped through the shut doors. When this happened, I held them open manually. While I was holding the doors open, I dropped my flashlight. I said to myself, "I hope it hits Hitler on the head."

As soon as the bombs were dropped, our pilot did what was called a corkscrew maneuver, and we got out of the lights. Later on, our co-pilot, Watson, who stayed in the Air Force, was flying a B-29 Bomber in the Korean War, and he used this maneuver to escape the searchlights there. (In 1957, Watson was killed in a B-29 crash in Georgia.)

We got back to base without anything happening and started a thirty-day wait for our trip back home to the US. While we were waiting for our orders, one day, one of our crews crash landed at our base. We never heard what happened to the crew; they were from another squadron.

On another day, two RAF pilots flying the British Spitfire fighter airplane landed at our base, and, after having lunch, took off. One of them did a loop and didn't pull out, and he hit a tree right next to our finance office. The pilot was killed instantly. The largest part of what was left of the plane was the engine.

The tree that the plane knocked down had to be moved, and someone found a crosscut saw for cutting it up. We sawed it up for firewood. Since we only got a bucket-full of coal each day, we could use the wood. Not many of the men had ever used a crosscut saw, but we had enough who knew how to use one to cut up the tree, and we made good use of that wood.

Before I left, I was awarded the "Air-Medal" with three oak-leaf clusters, and the "Distinguished Flying Cross", along with five campaign battle stars, a unit citation, and the French "Croix-Daguerre" for our group.

One morning we got our orders to go home. We were taken to another base to be scheduled to go home. We were there on Easter Sunday, 1945. When they got our crew of enlisted men together with personnel from other bases, we were taken to the railroad station at Worcester to be taken to Southampton to take a ship to the USA. The officers were taken to another camp. All officers with

"Distinguished Flying Cross" Awards Ceremony
Talmadge P. Fletcher, ASN 34604715

the rank of major and above could fly home, but the others had to take a ship. Finally, in late afternoon on April 5, 1945, I was put on a ship bound for home.

The Voyage Home

I was glad to be going home to the "good old USA." I wasn't worried about the German U-boats that were sinking a lot of our ships in the Atlantic

Ocean. The submarine patrol would take care of them.

It wasn't long before the evening meal was ready, and I was glad because I hadn't eaten for a long time. The meal was very good, because the Navy had good cooks. We had to hold our trays because they would slide down the metal table we ate on, and we had to eat standing up. It wasn't long afterwards when the good meal and I parted ways. As the old saying goes, "I was as sick as a buzzard." I thought I would get over being seasick, and I did — fourteen days later. I was glad then that I hadn't joined the Navy.

We were on a small ship that carried about five hundred passengers, and this was its first voyage, we were told. Its name was USS *General William Wiegal*. It had a sister ship that we were told was carrying a load of nurses. That must have been true because several of the officers who had binoculars were always watching it.

We stayed in the harbor for two days while a convoy of thirty-two ships was being made up, and then we finally headed for home. Someone told me to lie down, and it would help my seasickness. They were right because I did feel a little bit better after lying down.

We had pretty smooth sailing for a few days, and then we hit the spring storms that were in the North Atlantic Ocean. The storms lasted about three days. The big waves subsided, and then I felt a little better. One morning, April 12th, 1945, the ship's captain announced that President Roosevelt had died, and Harry S. Truman was now our President. Another morning, about two o'clock, we heard what we thought was depth charges, and one of the crew said that they were depth charges. One of the destroyer escorts was dropping depth charges at a U-Boat that was after the convoy. We never did find out what happened.

After fourteen days, I found the cure for my seasickness: It was the Statue of Liberty because I started to feel better when it came into view.

When we got off the ship, the landing area was surrounded by MPs. Someone said there were prisoners on board, and they might try to escape. They left them on the ship until we were gone and then retrieved them.

We were taken to the Fort Dix Army Base where they had a meal ready for us, but I went to the snack bar and had a milkshake. We were given orders that allowed us to go home on leave and told us our next duty station. In my case, I received orders to go to Santa Ana, California. I was supposed to go back to England for more missions after going there.

From Fort Dix, I rode down to Fort Bragg in a boxcar. The boxcars had bunks installed on the walls, and they were quite comfortable. There was a bunk for each of us on that train. I didn't mind the chance to rest because I was going home for at least a little while. I didn't know then that I wouldn't be going back to Europe.

The train was slow. It took all night to make the trip, but it was going in the right direction. From Fort Bragg to Canton, I rode a bus. It was not as good a ride as that boxcar, but it got me home.

Married

The first thing I did when I got back home was to go and see my sweetheart, Alveta Medford. I had been in love with her even when she didn't know it. When we moved back to Canton in 1938, I found that the men in the community had a softball team. They were playing across the hill from where we lived, and I went to watch them play, hoping they would let me play with them. I was lucky that day. Not only did I get to play ball, but I saw a pretty young girl there, and I hoped some day to make her my wife.

She didn't know it for a few years, but every time I walked past her house or saw her on the school bus, I had a little more love in my heart. I also had worked for her father, and I had gotten to eat lunch with her family. All the time, I hoped she would someday love a little old boy like me. I don't know exactly when it happened, but one day we both knew we were meant for each other.

When I was in the Army Air Corps during WWII, I tried to find time to write Alveta a letter now and then. I only got to see her one time since I joined the Army, and that was when I went home on emergency leave because my dad was in the hospital. My brother came home also, and he and I, and our future wives, had a good time taking a trip to the Smoky Mountains together. That week of emergency leave was soon over, and I went back to radio school.

When I got home from England, Alveta and I decided to get married. We were married at her home on May 3rd, 1945, by a preacher named Barnes who had never married anyone before. He did a good job, because the marriage lasted almost sixty-nine years.

After we were married, we caught the Trailways bus and went to Gatlinburg, Tennessee. We looked around for a place to stay, and we found a cabin in a tourist court. It was in a beautiful spot and was close to everything in Gatlinburg. We spent lots of time looking at all the attractions that were there then. There was a nice little café where we ate our breakfast each morning. We didn't tell them in the café that we were married, but they played a record, and some of the words to the song were, "I wanna

Newlyweds

get married and sleep in pajama tops." I guess they could tell that we were married.

After we had looked at everything in town, we went to Knoxville, Tennessee. I met an Army officer there, and when I saluted, I realized that I didn't have my cap on. (I had left it in our cabin.) Thankfully, the officer didn't notice or didn't care. There was a country music show in Knoxville called the "Mid-Day Merry-Go-Round." While we were watching the show, someone stopped it to announce that he had just heard that the war in Europe was over. The crowd really enjoyed the news. I was happy, too, because I knew I wouldn't have to go back to England.

Santa Ana, California

After my leave was over, I had to report to Santa Ana, California, for further orders. I caught the train in Asheville, North Carolina, and headed for Los Angeles, California. The train that took me to Cincinnati, Ohio, was called the "Carolina Special." I had to change trains there to go to Chicago, Illinois. I changed trains again in Chicago, where I started the last leg of the trip to Los Angeles.

I got to Los Angeles a day early and decided to visit my friend Robert (Bob) Sanchez in San Bernardino. He was home on his leave, also. He was glad that I came by, and his mother insisted that I spend the night even though she had a large family. She had twin sons, Bob's wife, and Bob already in the house, but she made room for me. Afterwards, she sent me a Christmas card every year until she died. Bob's father had died while we were in England.

The next day, Bob and I reported to Santa Ana Army Base to get further orders. After we reported and settled down, we were told that the mess hall was open, and we could eat any time we wanted to. I was really surprised at the food they had prepared for us. They had lots of meat and fish dishes, along with several other things, and as we were going out, we could get fruits that were provided for us. They also had a large building that stayed open until eleven o'clock at night where we could have ice cream, sandwiches, milk shakes, and all sorts of other snacking foods. We had never had it that good in the Army before.

There were several meetings we had to attend, and we were told that if we didn't miss any or arrive late for any, when we got to our new assignment we would be given a furlough. I made sure to be on time and not to miss a meeting.

We had heard on the news that those who had enough points could be given a discharge. The points were given for length of service and for medals. I was sure to get out, I thought, but I had two medals that were not on my record that I needed before I could be discharged. While I was there, my medals were added to my service record, but they told me it was too late, that I had already been ordered to go to another base.

I met man from another Army base who wanted me to go with him to his home in Hollywood. He had his father's car, and he said we would be back for our first meeting at seven o'clock the next morning. I asked him where we would get gasoline, and he said he could get plenty. I was persuaded to go. Besides, I didn't think I would ever get another chance to go to Hollywood.

Hollywood was seventy miles away, and when we got there, I saw that his home was what I would call a mansion. It had a very large room with a grand piano, which the man's cousin was playing when I arrived. There was a stable with two horses, and we went for a horseback ride (like the cowboys) when it got dark. He took me to a night-club that his father owned, and it had a crowd of customers. My friend told his father he needed some gas ration coupons, and he gave us plenty to get us back with.

I had never been nor have I ever been since in a place like this mansion. My luxury was short-lived, though, and I soon returned to my ordinary life. We were back in time for our meeting the next morning, and I had to leave for Louisiana the same day.

Selman Field

I received orders to go to Selman Field in Monroe, Louisiana. Three other Airmen were sent there, too. I was put in charge of the other men until we got to Selman Field. We caught a train which went to Fort Worth, Texas, where we needed to change trains. The other three men wanted to stay in Fort Worth until the next day, but I wouldn't let them. After all, I was responsible for them, and I would be the one to answer for their actions.

I checked the train schedule and was told which one was going to Monroe. We had to wait for about another hour before it left, and we walked around the station while we were waiting. When the train got to the station, we boarded and settled down in our reserved seats. We had sleeping berths, and it was night time, so we got in our berths and got some sleep.

The next morning about five o'clock, the conductor woke us up, took us to the end of the train (the caboose), and told us the train didn't go to Monroe, and that we had to get off somewhere else. About ten o'clock we were put off at a small station out in the country. I told the man who looked after the station that he should furnish us transportation to Monroe because it was not our fault — the station master in Fort Worth had put us on the wrong train. He said he would take care of us, and he got us a car to take us to the bus station, and he paid our fare. After another thirty-mile ride, we finally made it to Monroe, where we caught a ride to Selman Field.

The airbase was used for training navigators. There were several types of aircraft in use there: the C46, C47, AT-7, and AT-11. Our job was to fly with students while they practiced. After a few days, they were true to their word, because I was given a two-week furlough.

The bus ride back home took thirty hours, and when I got to Canton I was asleep. By the time I woke up, I saw that I was past Canton, and I told the bus driver to let me off. I was about two miles past Canton and was wondering how I could walk and carry my luggage. Then I got lucky. A bus that carried workers to the paper factory was coming back from its trip, and it stopped and picked me up. The driver was going past where I was going, to the home where my new bride lived with her parents. The bus dropped me off at my father-in-law's house. I was glad to be there, and I awakened everyone before going to bed.

One morning I wanted to help with the milking of two cows. Alveta's dad said I would get my uniform dirty if I milked the cows, but I insisted on doing it. When I had almost a bucket-full of milk, the cow I was milking kicked and splashed milk all over my new gabardine uniform. I took the uniform to the dry cleaners, and they finished ruining it.

After a few days of my leave passed, I got sick with what I thought was the "flu" and had to stay in bed for a week of my furlough. I survived, though, and I got well enough to go back to Selman Field.

While I was helping train students, we flew around the country, and we sometimes stayed overnight in various places. One time, we stayed at Avon Park, Florida, and I was eaten up by mosquitoes. Later on, I had malaria, and I think that was where I caught it.

Another thing happened on that trip: A corporal on one of the other crews was married, and his wife came to see him while we were in Florida. We had stayed all night somewhere because of bad weather, and when we started back to Monroe the next morning, we were caught in a thunderstorm. The airplane that the corporal was on crashed and killed all thirteen men aboard, and the corporal never got to see his wife again.

We were often told that weather was our worst enemy. We kept training student navigators. In addition to going on training flights, I was put in charge of the radio group, and we had to do preflight checks of the radios on every plane. We were pretty busy when not flying, too.

One morning the headlines in the paper told of the dropping of the atomic bomb, and we figured that Japan would surely surrender. But, it took a second city being destroyed before they did. At that point, we figured that it wouldn't be long before the war in the Pacific was over. That was in August. I was discharged the next month, on September 15, 1945.

Back to Fort Bragg

Everyone was being discharged according to seniority and where they were to be discharged from. I was being sent back to Fort Bragg, the place where I was inducted. When my day came, I was told that I had never been qualified to shoot the forty-five caliber pistol, and I couldn't be discharged until I did. I had to report to the firing range the next morning and qualify. The reason I never qualified was that I never had to go through Basic Training, and I only had the chance to shoot skeet with a shotgun and to use the fifty-caliber machine guns that were on the aircraft.

The next morning I reported to the range, and it didn't take long to qualify, and now the qualification could be put on my service record. I don't know what I would have done during our combat missions if I had been in a place where I had to shoot a pistol.

I found out that it wasn't my time yet to be discharged, because someone else from Canton had more points than I did, and he was scheduled to go back before I did. I later found out that he told them to let me go in his place, and that he would go next time. The reason was that he had a girlfriend there, and he didn't want to leave her at that time. I didn't know him then, but when I went to work after I got home, I found out that he was married. I never told anyone because he allowed me to go home earlier than I would have. Later, he and his wife were divorced.

I finally had my orders, and I was going home. I was sent to a camp in Livingston, Louisiana, where I spent the night, and the next day I went on to Fort Bragg, along with another man. I wasn't the only one there to be discharged, and I had to stay a few days.

There were several men in my group at Ft Bragg, and one of them cursed the Army for everything that they did. One day, we had gravy for dinner, and he went back for seconds and was told that the gravy was all gone. When he got back to the table, he cursed the Army some more and said he could take a sack of flour and make enough gravy to feed the whole Army himself.

When our time came to leave, we were sent to the mess hall to get our final meal, after which our discharges would be ready. We were told that if we would re-enlist, we would be given a rank above what we had, but no one took them up on the offer. When we went back to get our discharges, the man who had cursed the Army so much was missing, and the sergeant in charge asked if anyone knew where he was. Someone said that he had re-enlisted. We learned that he didn't have a home to go to. His only living family was a sister, and he had nowhere to go. The rest of us got our discharges, got on a bus, and finally headed home.

Civilian Life

Thickety Again

It was midnight by the time we got discharged and got on the bus, so it was the next day when I got off the bus. Since I wanted to go home as a civilian, I went to Nicholls Men's Clothing Store, where I bought a suit and a hat. While I waited for the suit to be adjusted, I went to a barber shop and got a haircut, a shave, and a massage. When I got back to the clothing store, the suit was ready, and I changed into civilian clothing. I headed to Thickety as a civilian, and when Alveta opened the door to her house and saw me, I believe she thought I was a peddler.

When we got through with all the home-coming, I started life as a civilian. Alveta had been working in the local paper mill, and she had bought a little house from her father, so we set about moving into it. She had rented it to a couple while I was gone, and we had to wait for them to move before we could do anything. I had been saving all the money the Army would let me, and it was enough to buy our furniture and other things we needed to start housekeeping. I needed a job, so I went to the Champion Paper Mill and applied for one. I didn't have to wait long — I was hired right away.

There are lots of different things that go into to making paper. I'll try to explain what it takes in simple words. The first thing is wood. In the past, it was brought to the mill in five-foot sections and then cut into chips about three-quarters of an inch long. Those chips are then sent to a large tank, where they are cooked into a pulp. The pulp is then sent through a screening process, followed by a bleaching process, and then on to the paper machine. At the paper machine, the pulp goes into a head box, which spreads the pulp onto a part of the machine called "the wire." There, most of the water is taken out by vacuum pumps. The thin layer of pulp then goes through a smoothing process followed by going through a series of dryers that are heated by steam. Next it goes through a series of rollers and is rolled up into a large roll. Finally, the large roll is re-wound and cut into the different sizes customers want.

I wanted to earn the living for us, so Alveta quit her job at the mill and started her new job keeping house. I was given a job working with the Labor Crew. I worked hard at any job I was given, but I was hoping for another kind of work to spend the rest of my working life at. One day, one of the men who had known me since I was a young boy stopped me while I was pushing a wheelbarrow. He told me I was working too hard and that if I worked hard, I would never get a transfer to another job. I said if I didn't work hard, nobody else would want me. He was right, though, because the men who would not do their part but would sit or lie down when the boss was not around, got a better job. Yet, when I had two different chances to get a better job, the Labor Crew wouldn't let me go.

I ate a lot while I was in the Army Air Corps, but I never did get fat. I lost one pound and weighed 137 pounds when I was discharged. I didn't gain any weight until I was about 45 years old. When I went to work in the paper mill, I got the nick-name "Bones" because I was tall and thin. A lot of the workers used my nick-name and never called me by my real name.

I wanted to buy a car to drive to work. We got an hour for lunch, and one day I left the mill and went to where they issued driver's licenses. I got my driver's license, and then I went to a used car lot that was close by and bought an old 1938 Chevrolet. I still made it back to work on time. It wasn't the best car in the world, but it took me to and from work. When the weather got below freezing, I had to use hot water to thaw out the carburetor.

Charles wanted me to take him to Clayton, Georgia, to get married. So, one day, Charles, Marie Young (his bride), and Alveta were ready to go to Georgia when I got off work at four o'clock in the evening. It was a cold day in February, and we had to cross a mountain where we were met by heavy snow. Thankfully, it stopped snowing after we got across the mountain. Then the road was clear of snow after that, and we made it to Clayton without any trouble. We found the Justice of the Peace, and when we went in to his office, we saw another couple who were from Canton getting married. After Charles and Marie completed their wedding vows, we all went on to Atlanta where we were going to spend the night.

I wanted to go to a country music show in Atlanta, but I never found the location of the show. While I was looking for it, I was almost run over by a streetcar that was in operation in Atlanta at that time. My car didn't have good brakes, and the clutch slipped, but I got out of the way of the streetcar just in time to avoid being hit. Alveta and I came home the next morning, and we left Charles and Marie in Georgia. My old car had made it to Georgia and back.

When I found that the Coyne Electrical School of Chicago was advertising for students, I applied and was accepted. I went to talk to my superintendent at the paper mill and told him about my plan to go to school, and I asked him for a leave of absence. He told me he didn't blame me for wanting to quit my job to get more training but that he couldn't give me a leave for the length of time I needed. He told me to work a two-week resignation notice and to come back to him when I was out of school, and he would do what he could for me to help me get rehired. Most of the workers were afraid of him, but I found him to be a good supervisor. He knew who worked and who didn't.

Chicago, Illinois

When I decided to go to school, I was going to use the "GI Bill" (the Servicemen's Readjustment Act of 1944) to help with my expenses. I needed to go to Asheville to sign up for it. When I got there, I found a long line of others waiting for the same thing, and I thought I would have to wait a long time. A few minutes later, someone said, "What are you doing here?"

It was my teacher from high school, Mr. Donovan, who taught me to do metal working and to be a machinist. When I told him what I wanted, he said, "Come with me," and he took me ahead of all the others to his office to sign me up. He wanted me to go to a school in Milwaukee, Wisconsin, but I told him I didn't have the background for that. He signed me up for the GI Bill, and after I worked a two-week notice at the mill, I was ready to go. Alveta's dad even found me a buyer for my car.

When my brother Charles found that I was going to Coyne Electrical School, he decided he wanted to go as well. I gave him the application form to send to the school, and they accepted him. They let him take the place of someone who had dropped out, and he got to go three weeks before I went. That worked out well for me because he found us a place to live that was close enough for us to walk to school. It was not the fanciest place in Chicago, but it served our needs.

When we were all set, Alveta, Marie (Charles's wife), and I caught the bus in Canton and headed to the big city of Chicago. First, we had to go to

Knoxville, Tennessee, and change to another bus. We left Knoxville, and after about an hour the bus broke down. We had to wait about another hour for another bus to come to our aid. The other bus that came to our aid was a new one that didn't have all the modifications it needed done yet, but it was the only one available. So, we got to ride a new bus to Chicago. We didn't have any more trouble after that, and we arrived safely.

The landlord of our new apartment met us at the bus station and took us to the place that was to be our home while we were going to school. We had quite a time adjusting to our living quarters, but we did the best we could. We didn't have a lot of money to spend for a better place, even if it could be found.

The first night there, Alveta woke up and said something had bitten her. I got up and found bedbugs. Alveta had never seen one, but I knew what they were. The next day, we told the landlord about them, but he said there were no bedbugs in his apartments.

I had seen bedbugs before, but they didn't bite me. (I guess I was too tough). I knew how to get rid of them. I bought some moth ball powders and kerosene and mixed them together. I painted the bed springs and the baseboards with the mixture, and we shut the door of the bedroom and left for the day. When we came back, we opened the window and aired out the room. It didn't smell too good for a few days, but we never saw another bedbug there.

We went looking for another apartment on a Sunday afternoon, but we never found one. We went to one place where we found a couple painting. When we asked the man about where he went to church, he said, "I couldn't go today — I have to paint. But, I sent in my donation envelope." We didn't find another place, so we decided to stop looking and stay where we were since we had killed the bedbugs.

Alveta and Marie set out to look for a job, and they found one at a place that made watches. Their jobs helped to pay our expenses. They were told by one of the tenants not to ever go out alone, because it wasn't safe. They advised us at school to put our money in the vault at school, or otherwise we stood a chance of being robbed. One student was followed, then when he got off the bus at a place that was not crowded, the man who followed him there robbed him, and as a result, he didn't have enough money to stay in school.

We got along pretty well financially with Alveta and Marie working. I got to go to watch the Chicago Cubs play baseball. I also got to see a favorite pitcher, Bob Feller, at the White Sox Comiskey Park. We got to see the zoo and museum of natural history, among other places of interest.

One day, Alveta and I went to an amusement park. We were strolling around, looking at all the rides and other attractions, and after watching the rollercoaster, Alveta said, "Let's take a ride on it!" I said, "OK, let's go!" I thought she would get scared, but when it stopped, she wanted to ride again.

We went to an Army Day celebration, and they had a lot of speeches and other patriotic things. There were so many things going on in jam-packed Soldier Field that it was hard to get around. But, we could see the flyovers the Army Air Corps made. It took awhile to get through the crowd, but we finally got out.

Before we knew it, Charles was through school, and he and Marie were going home. I had three more weeks of school, and after Charles and Marie left, Alveta and I moved to another apartment that had been vacated by another couple on the bottom floor. It was better place than what we had before.

Three weeks passed by quickly, and we packed and caught the bus for home.

Back to Thickety (final time)

We arrived home on the weekend, and when I saw Charles at church that Sunday, he told me he was going to work at the paper mill the next day. I realized then that Mr. Stone had given him the job meant for me. The next day, I went to the YMCA where all the managers ate lunch in a dining room upstairs, and I waited for the managers to come downstairs.

When Mr. Stone saw me, he told the employment manager, "There is the man I told you to hire. He has been going to the electrical school."

Mr. McElrath said, "The one I hired went to the same school, and I didn't know the difference between them. What do you want me to do?"

Mr. Stone said, "Hire this one, too. We can use them both."

Charles and I both worked hard, and I suppose we were noticed, because every time one of us asked for a raise, we both got one.

When we first went to work with the electricians, there were about sixty men in the Electrical

Department. The mill installed three paper machines, and I worked on all of them at times. When the last one was installed, I was given the job of coordinating all the electrical work that the contractors did on the job. After the machines started making paper, I was promoted to a foreman's job. I then looked after all the electrical work on all the machines. I later was given the general foreman's job. I was responsible for the whole Electrical Department and for the Instrument Section, also.

After I retired, I was called on to go back to work on a special project with a long-time friend, Ray Whitted. He is retired now, and he is the only electrician still alive who was in the Department when I joined it. He and I meet at the Canton Burger King every Friday morning for breakfast and talk of the things that once were.

Charles and I both went to all the night classes that the mill offered, and we tried to learn all we could. At one time, I went to four classes each week. The classes ranged from English, taught by one of the English professors at a college close by, to electronics. We also had blueprint reading and paper machine operation. I ended up getting thirty-three certificates for completing classes. In the meantime, I went to Raleigh, North Carolina, and took the examination for an electrical contracting license and was awarded my license. I did a lot of house wiring and repairs in my spare time. Later on, I taught a course on paper machine electrical drives. I also taught another class at the Haywood Community College that was called, "Troubleshooting Electrical Machinery."

Family

After we got home from Chicago and settled down, we went about trying to buy things for the house. Such things as a washing machine, a refrigerator, and an automobile were not readily available at that time, and you had to get on a list and wait for your turn to purchase one. I was on a waiting list at every store in town.

One day, Alveta's uncle asked if we had bought a refrigerator. She told him that we hadn't, and he told us that two different stores in town had one available for him, and we could buy one of them. That was in 1947. So, we were lucky, but it was another year before we got a washing machine, and it was 1952 before I got a new car.

I had my name on the waiting list for an automobile at three places: the Chevrolet, Plymouth, and Ford dealers. I was checking one day, and a man at the Ford place let me have a car that had just come in. It wasn't like it is today. Back then, you had to pay one-third of the price up front, not like today when you buy on credit and make a payment each month.

Through marriage, I became a member of a close-knit extended family. The three men who married three girls from Wilson and Dixie Medford's family and our wives were all very close. Howard Dotson married Edith, who was the oldest Medford girl; I married Alveta, who was the middle girl; and Hugh Early married Jennie Mae, the youngest Medford girl. We did a lot of things together as families, and I don't remember any one of us ever saying anything against any other member of our related families.

Jennie Mae, Alveta, Edith, Dixie, and Wilson Medford

We finally got the things we needed for our household, and we decided it was time to raise a family. After I was back to work for about a year, this time with the mill's Electric Department, a son, Robert Alan, was born on November 20th, 1947.

I wasn't a Christian at that time, but I went to church with Alveta. I sang the old hymns and thought I was a pretty good person. Revival meetings were being held at the Oak Grove Baptist Church in February of 1949. I had been attending most nights, but I had to stay home on Saturday night and keep Robert while Alveta went to keep her sister's baby.

I was listening to the radio that night, and I felt that something was telling me to go to church. I got Robert ready and took him to Alveta, and I told her I was going to church. When the altar call was made, I was the first one to go forward, and I asked God to forgive me from all my sins and wrong-doings. That Saturday night, February 19, 1949, I became a Christian. After that, I lived my life so that I would be someone that my family would be proud of, and all of my children and grandchildren have become Christians. I love them all for who they are to their children.

Oak Grove Baptist Church

On April 15th, 1952, our daughter, Cathy Sue, was born. She had what was called the "three month colic", when a baby cried all night and slept all day. However, Cathy cried all day and slept all night. After that phase, she was a good little girl and never caused any trouble.

When Robert got old enough, he went with me to the garden and kept me company. Every year we always made a big garden where we grew vegetables for ourselves and the extended family.

When Robert was six years old and Cathy was a baby, we went on vacation to Charleston, South Carolina. When we got there, it was getting dark, and we started to look for a motel and couldn't find one. They were not as plentiful then as they are now. We had to find a place to stay soon in order to take care of the children, so we couldn't be picky. We ended up checking into a big hotel.

We had packed our things in boxes instead of suitcases. We had to carry our boxes to our room and let someone park our car. I'm not sure what they thought of us, but I didn't care. We paid for our room and for parking valet service. I don't know what they expected in the way of tips, but I guess they got more than they expected. We never found a motel that we wanted to stay in, so after we ate breakfast the next morning, we drove back home to Thickety. We later realized that we had left Robert's suit coat in the restaurant where we ate breakfast.

When Robert was in school, he played Little League baseball, and I enjoyed watching his games. By the time he went to high school, he joined the football team, and I took him to practice and watched him play every game but one, when I was away on business. I was proud of him then and am proud of him now.

Once, when he was in the eighth grade, he and his friend, Doug Buchanan, got off the school bus in town and walked the rest of the way. It was about Easter time, and they stopped at the Farmers Federation store, and each of them bought a little chicken. When they got to school, they put the chickens in their lockers. Someone heard them cheeping and told a teacher, who made a big deal out of it and called both boys' parents to come and get them. Doug and Robert were close friends, and I always took Doug along everywhere that Robert went. They also played football together. Now, they both have retired and live in the same community in eastern North Carolina, and they play golf together.

When the boys were in the Royal Ambassadors program at church, they went on a trip to the Great Smoky Mountains National Park. While they were there, a small black bear came to where the boys were staying, and Robert caught it and put it in a trash can. He was lucky that the mama bear wasn't close by. I didn't know about that incident until years later.

One time I took a group of boys to the Linville Caverns. On the way home, it was raining hard, and I slid into a ditch to keep from hitting the car in front of me. The boys were thrilled to have been in a car wreck.

I put a basketball hoop on the front of my garage, and several of the boys would come to play.

When the teams were unbalanced, I would play until someone else came. I was playing one day, and as I stopped suddenly, I turned my ankle and broke my toe. The doctor told me to quit playing basketball.

When Cathy was in high school, she was in the school band. I got to go with the band as a chaperone when they travelled, and I enjoyed the trips. We would sing all the way. I think I enjoyed the trips as much as they did.

Once, we had a Nativity scene at church, and I borrowed a donkey for the scene. That summer, the donkey's owners went out of town for a few weeks, and we kept the donkey all summer. Cathy and her friends played with it, and when they tried to ride it, the donkey wouldn't move. They tried and tried to get it to move, but Aunt Sukey the donkey just wasn't good transportation.

When Cathy was asked when she first learned about Jesus, she said, "I always knew. My daddy always read my Sunday school lesson to me before I could read." We always had a family altar in our home where we read the Bible and prayed.

Every summer while Robert and Cathy were growing up, we took them to the beach. Howard and his family, and Hugh and his family always

Cathy on Sukey

joined us — we were one big happy family. Howard, Hugh, and I fished and hunted together, and we all worked at the paper mill while raising our families.

One year, my family, Howard's family, and Troy Willis's family all went to the beach together. We rented a house large enough for all of us. One morning, Troy asked if Howard and me if we wanted to go deep-sea fishing. I said that I didn't want to go because I would get seasick.

Troy said, "You won't get sick! It is just a fishing boat. It won't be like a big ship."

I let him talk me into going, but I told him I wanted to go by the drugstore first to see if they had something to keep me from getting seasick. We went to the drugstore and asked for seasickness medicine. The druggist was a retired Navy pharmacist, so I thought that if anyone knew of a cure, it would be him. I said, "Are you sure that this medicine will keep me from being sick?"

He answered, "Nobody has ever complained yet!"

I said, "Okay, I'll take some."

He instructed me to take one pill when I got on the boat and another pill an half-hour later. Then he said that when I was out on the water and felt woozy, I could take another pill, and I would be all right.

I took his advice, and I was still on the boat waiting to start the trip when it came time for my second pill. I was feeling woozy already, and I went to get some water to drink with the pill. At the water faucet, I met another seasick victim who couldn't hold back. Seeing that sure didn't help me, and I joined him in vomiting.

After that, I was determined not to get sick anymore, but that didn't work. I was able to stay well only long enough to catch two fish. When I looked around for Howard, I saw that he had already given up fishing and was down on the deck with his head over the side, feeding the fish instead of catching them. I laid my fishing pole down and joined him. Troy didn't get sick, and he said that Howard and I were as green as gourds.

We lived through the fishing trip and got back alive, and the next morning I went to the drugstore and asked for the man who sold me the pills. The druggist told me that the man was off work that day. I asked him if he would give him a message, and he asked me what I wanted to tell him. I said, "Tell him the reason nobody has ever complained is because nobody has ever returned!"

After we returned to our lodgings, while I was waiting for Howard, I was reading the *Reader's Digest*, and one of the first things I saw was an article about a new cure for motion sickness. It didn't matter to me because I didn't need the cure now.

During our working years at Champion International Paper Corporation, Howard and I rode to work together. We rode a work bus for awhile, and then we bought a car together and drove it to work and back. When we wore it out, we decided to get rid of it, so I drove it to a junkyard and sold it for $25.

Howard and I fished together, and one year we went to a little lake that we had been to before, Lake Adger. It was cold that morning (I think it was February), and though we did a lot of fishing, we never had a bite. We fished until about ten o'clock in the morning and then decided to move to another lake nearby, Lake Lure.

We went across Lake Lure and fished until late in the afternoon; yet, here again we never got a bite. We decided to call it a day. We had only a small fishing engine, and we were afraid to try going back across the lake because there were some big boats racing up and down where we had to cross. We waited until we got a chance, and then we went across. We saw in the newspaper the next day that someone who was racing in Lake Lure the day before had wrecked his boat and drowned.

We didn't give up on fishing. Another day when we got off work, we went to another lake, Lake Chatuge. We fished all day, and again we never got a bite. We gave up this time and waited until warmer weather before we went fishing again. We went back to Lake Chatuge when it was warmer and fished all night for pike.

One night, Howard, JR Sorrells, and I went pike fishing, and we came upon a school of fish that were just barely too short to legally catch. Every one we caught that night was about 14 ¾ inches long, and the legal size was 15 inches or larger. When JR or I caught fish that were too short, we threw them back into the water. When Howard caught one, he kept it.

When Howard saw us throwing our fish back, he said he wanted to keep them. I reminded him that a man was caught a few days ago who had two fish that were too short, and they took his fishing equipment and fined him $40. I told Howard that I didn't want to be caught with any fish that were illegal. He said he didn't care, and he kept all the fish on his string. When we ran out of bait at about 4:00 AM, Howard had thirty illegal fish, and JR and I had nineteen large, legal ones. We split the small ones open so that if we saw the Game Warden, we could throw them overboard and they would sink.

When we started to go home, we saw a boat that shined a big spotlight on us from pretty close by. I let the string that had the short fish on it loose, and it sank out of sight. When I did that, the boat with the spotlight turned the light off and stopped. When we went to the car to go home, there was

Memories from Thickety

JR, Howard, and me the night that we threw thirty fish away

a man there who wanted to see our fish. We were pretty sure he had been told to check our catch. JR and I were always sure that the person on the boat with the spotlight and the man in the parking lot were Game Wardens, but Howard never did believe they were, and he regretted that I threw his fish away. We always enjoyed fishing, though.

There is a resort town in Haywood County, North Carolina, called Maggie Valley. It sits at the foot of a mountain. After WWII, someone bought the mountain and built a tourist attraction on top of it and named it "Ghost Town in the Sky." One day, our entire family went there to enjoy the shows about the Old West that Ghost Town put on. Wilson and Dixie, Alveta and I, Robert and Cathy, Howard and Edith and their three children, Linda, Lee Anna, and Mary Frances, and Hugh and Jennie Mae and their three children, Tommy, Darlene, and Ricky were all there that day.

At that time, there were two rides that carried people to the top of the mountain. One was a bus that went around a winding road, and the other was an inclined railroad that went straight up the mountain. The day we went, the railroad was broken down, and we rode the bus. It seemed like we would never get to the top, but we finally did.

Once were on top of the mountain, we saw saloons, can-can dancing, gunfights, and other things that were like they had been in the Old West. Ghost Town had an actor portraying Wyatt Earp, the sheriff of the town. Robert said that he outdrew Wyatt in a gun fight.

After we saw all the sights and were ready to leave, an attendant told us that the railroad was ready to run and that we could ride it instead of the bus if we wanted to. We decided to try it out.

All seventeen of us gave it a trial run, and it was better than the bus. I thought, "If this thing fails, it will wipe out our entire family." It also would have knocked a big hole in the population of Thickety, too, but we all survived.

One thing that stands out in my mind every Christmas is the fact that I never got a toy for Christmas while I was growing up. All we ever got for Christmas was maybe an orange and a stick of hard candy. For my own children, we always tried to get them something comparable to what their friends were getting. In the first years of my work at the mill, I had to work every holiday. So, I had to play Santa Claus at all different hours at Christmas; but Santa never failed to come to our house.

I guess I was loved as a child, but I don't ever remember being told that I was loved by my father. Instead of being a giver, he was a taker. When I was in the Service, I sent money home to him to save for me, but he always took it for himself. Finally, I started sending my money straight to the bank where it was safe.

We decided to build a new and larger house, and when it was time for me to do the wiring, I got sick. I worked until I had double pneumonia to get the house to the point where the carpenters would not cover my work. I had to go to bed until I got better. My doctor sent his nurse on a house-call to give me my medicine. I got well, but Alveta was worn out by doing the things that had to be done while I was sick.

We moved into our new house and lived there until we decided to build another house. In my new house I wanted to have a large basement where I could keep my car. While we were building this house, I was working at the mill, so Alveta looked after the building project and did a lot of the little things that had to be done each day. She and Cathy did most of the painting in the house, and I did the electrical work.

Cathy Sue

Robert Alan

Our house in 1980 — I still live here.

After the house was built and we were settled in, we decided to put a wood burning stove in the fireplace, which meant we needed wood. We had plenty of wood around, but it had to be cut and hauled to the house. I bought a yard tractor and a cart, and together we formed a team — I would saw and split the wood, and Alveta would haul it to the house. She did everything she could do to help me while I was working at the mill or wiring somebody's house. We had a good time helping each other.

During the years after WWII, the government encouraged country communities to have a program where the people got together and shared things to help each other. We had dinner meetings along with sports. We had softball teams, horseshoe pitching, and basketball teams. We competed with each other, and it was good for us to meet each other, but that gradually came to an end. Some of the communities still have their own activities and programs. Our community still kept a softball team for a few more years. After that team was no longer active, I joined the paper mill Maintenance Department team. I stayed on that team until I became too slow to play well.

During my years as a member of the Oak Grove Baptist Church, I stayed active in the church by being a deacon and by teaching Sunday school classes. I taught pupils ranging from small children to the oldest members, who, when they leave the class for their age, go on to a class in the sky.

I was the church Song Leader for a few years until we felt the need to have an organized choir and hired a Music Director. We have had several of them through the years, and we have been blessed by their talents. At this time, we have an excellent one, Bill Terrell.

After Robert graduated from Asheville-Buncombe Technical College, he moved to Boone,

North Carolina, where he went to work for a company that made resistors for the electronics industry called IRC. After he had been there a few months, he met a girl who worked in the plant, Diane Miller. They fell in love with each other and were married at a little church in Boone called "Meat Camp Baptist Church." It was called that because Daniel Boone once made a camp where the church is located. He married the best wife he could ever find. Diane is a wonderful person and is as close to us as our own children. They joined Perkinsville Baptist Church in Boone. The pastor at the time was brother Allard, and Robert was a deacon in the church.

When Robert and Diane built their house, I spent several weekends driving to Boone to do the wiring for them. After a few years, their son, Eric, was born. Then, Robert's company sent him to Corpus Christi, Texas, where their son, Ryan, was born. After four years there, he was sent him to Los Angeles, California, and after a few more years, his employer sent him to Dallas, Texas.

Alveta and I went to visit Robert's family every Thanksgiving that we could, and they came to see us for a week or two in the summer every couple of years. Now that their boys are grown and have families of their own, Robert and Diane have moved to Cary, North Carolina, so I see them more often now. They are now members of Westwood Baptist Church, and their pastor is brother Allard, the same pastor they had in Boone so many years ago.

After Cathy graduated from Asheville-Buncombe Technical College, she married a pharmacist, Jeff DeWeese, and they moved to Chapel Hill, North Carolina, while he finished school. After he graduated, they moved to Asheville, North Carolina, where my other two grandchildren, Amy and Keith, were born.

Retirement

During the passing years, my wife, Alveta, and I have been blessed by living in what we believe to be one of the best communities in America and in the best family. If someone has a need, someone is quick to answer.

We were also blessed by having a pastor, Preacher Bruce Cayton, who was first to answer the needs of anyone, no matter when or where something was needed. One time he went to where a house was on fire, and he saw a young boy who had to leave the burning house barefoot. He pulled his own shoes off and gave them to the boy. It was in the dead of winter. Bruce is truly a man of God, and he is blessed by having one of the best ladies that ever was for his wife, Patsy. She is a beautiful person, and she has worked tirelessly along with Preacher Bruce for thirty-one years, after which he retired.

After I retired, the bomber group that I was with during WWII, the Carpetbaggers, had a reunion in Las Vegas, Nevada. Alveta and I planned to attend the reunion, and we wanted Jennie Mae and Hugh to go with us. We all drove from North Carolina to Las Vegas, and when we arrived, I checked to see who was there that I knew. After finding the people I knew, we ate lunch at one of the casinos.

Jennie Mae wanted to go on to California. We went to the Hoover Dam, to the Grand Canyon, to the Petrified Forest, and then to California. We went to the Sequoia National Forest and enjoyed seeing the big trees — one of them is supposed to be the oldest tree in the world. After spending the night in Bakersfield, California, we went to Carlsbad Caverns and enjoyed the trip through them. After the reunion was over, we drove to Dallas, Texas, and visited Robert. We stayed overnight and then headed back to Thickety. We had a wonderful time.

One summer, our neighbors, the Buchanan family — Hasting and Christine, their sons Doug and Billy, and their daughter Cathy — invited all of our families (Howard's, Hugh's, and mine) to spend the weekend at their cabin on the Cherokee Indian Reservation. The women stayed in the cabin, while Christine's brother, Jerome, took the men on a trip back into the Great Smoky Mountains to fish in a stream.

After we walked for what I think was several miles, Jerome led us down the mountainside to a stream of water. We waded the water and after another mile or so came to a place to camp for the night. Jerome told us we were not supposed to be in that area, but that we would be okay. He had an axe, and he cut wood for us, and we made a big fire to keep the bears away. I was the chef, and I cooked supper. After talking until midnight, we got into our sleeping bags and slept (I think) until daylight.

I cooked breakfast for us, and everyone but me went fishing. I stayed to clean up and take care of the camp. After two or three hours, the weary fishermen came back with the morning catch. They had caught ninety-six small trout. We packed up and started back to the cabin, and when we got to the top of the ridge and back onto the trail, Jerome told us that if we saw someone wearing green clothes, it would be a forest ranger, and we should go off the trail down the mountain a certain way, and that we could get back to the cabin that way.

It had to happen, of course. We saw someone in a green outfit, and everyone except Hugh started down the side of the mountain. I stayed with Jerome. He left his fishing pole and said he would get it later. We all got back to the cabin except for Hugh.

The person in the green outfit turned out to be a Boy Scout who was lost. When we arrived at the cabin, Jennie Mae wanted to know why we ran off and left Hugh by himself. At about that time, Hugh arrived with the Boy Scout. Jerome said he had better take the boy back to where he had started from, and when they got there, a ranger was organizing a search party to go looking for him. Jerome's brother knew we were on the mountain, and he was going to lead the search party in order to keep us from getting caught. It ended well because we got the boy back just in time. What happened on this trip has been told over and over again. It is one trip I don't want to forget.

For sixty-nine years, I was blessed with a wife who was easy to get along with. While I was working at the mill or for someone else, she did everything she could to help me.

As I mentioned before, I made a big garden every year, and we made a place in the basement of our house for canning our vegetables. What we didn't can, we gave away. We did this so that our children could have all they wanted because they lived where they couldn't make a garden of their own.

Alveta helped keep the yard mowed and kept the weeds out of the garden. One day, she was mow-

Alveta and me

ing the yard, and she stopped for dinner. When she returned to finish mowing, she started the mower, and when she moved it, she found a cut-up snake. It was a harmless black snake, but it was still a snake. She was always looking out for snakes when she was outside after that.

One time when my grandson, Keith, was small, he was playing in the yard, and he suddenly ran inside. He was all agitated, and he said, "Nanny, Nanny! There is a snake out in the yard, and it is a big one too!" He was right, because there was a big black snake out there. He and his sister, Amy, watched as I got the dog and a hoe, and I chopped its head off.

After I retired from the paper mill I started taking my surplus vegetables to the local tailgate market that was started so people with gardens could go and fellowship with others. I found it to be an enjoyable place to meet and get to know my neighbors. It also made a good place to witness to them about their relationship with God. After several years, it got to be more of a job than a hobby, and I started making a smaller garden and did more canning.

When the grandchildren were growing up, we brought Amy and Keith home with us to stay for a few days from time to time. Since they lived closer than Eric and Ryan did, we could do that more often with them. When they came, I would show them my garden plants and tell them what they were since most kids nowadays have never seen what vegetables look like while they're growing.

One time I had Keith for a few days, and as I was gathering my things to take to the Tailgate Market, I told him that if he would pick some beans, I would take them and sell them, and he could have the money I got for them. After a little while, he stopped picking, and I asked why he had stopped. He said he was going to pick them at his leisure. I tried to tell him that they needed picking then so that I could load them on the truck. Together, we finally got them picked, and I sold them and gave him the money.

Another time when I had some cantaloupes that were ripe, I told Keith and Amy that if they would take them down to the road and put up a sign, they could sell the cantaloupes to people passing by and could keep the money they got for selling them. They did that, and they made themselves some money that day.

I didn't have as many chances to do those kinds of things with Eric and Ryan, but I really enjoyed all of our visits to see them and their visits to see us during their vacations. Before they moved to Texas, I had the opportunity to keep Eric, and one time he got a jar and tried to catch fireflies to take home with him. Also, during one visit to Texas while Eric was in school, I went to pick him up from school, and he told everyone, "That is my grandpa!" One little boy said, "So what?" Eric was proud of his grandpa, and I was proud of him.

The last two or three years, Alveta couldn't go down the basement stairs, so I would take her down to the lower driveway in the car, and she took care of what she could while sitting down. When canning tomatoes, the tomatoes had to be scalded in hot water, and then the skin would come off. I would scald them, and she would take the skins off. Then I would put them into the jars that I had washed and put them into the canning pot and watch until they were done. Then I would take Alveta back upstairs. Alveta could make her jellies in our kitchen where she could sit down and let me do the stirring. She also made pickled beets that she enjoyed sharing with our pastor, Preacher Bruce.

We did a little better when we canned our cornfield beans. Alveta didn't have to go to the basement for that. I would pick the beans, and she could sit on the porch while she stringed and broke them into short pieces. I would wash the jars and help with the stringing and breaking, and then when we got enough fixed for a run (enough for seven quart-sized or nine pint-sized jars), I would take them to the basement and finish the canning. We tried to can enough for the children and grand-children. In one of our best years the garden produced a good crop of beans and tomatoes, and we canned 110 cans of tomatoes and 94 cans of beans.

One time when Robert's family was visiting, all four of my grandchildren wanted to ride in my yard tractor's trailer. I loaded them into the cart and took them on a drive around the garden. They wanted me to go faster, and when I turned the corner, they all slid to one side and turned the cart over. No one got hurt — Ryan and Amy were able to jump out before the cart completely turned over, and everyone else slid out and landed on the grass. They wanted to ride some more, but I was afraid someone might get hurt, so I stopped hauling them.

All of the grandchildren are grown now, and none of them live nearby anymore. Eric and his wife, Maria, live in Lynchburg, Virginia, with their children, Anna, Laura, and Reid. Ryan and his wife, Robyn, live outside of Dallas, Texas, with their children, Hayden and Lily. Keith and his wife, Tara, live outside of Raleigh, North Carolina, with their children, Kyle and Michelle. And Amy, our only granddaughter, lives outside of Nashville, Tennessee. All of them are active in their churches. We have loved our grandchildren and their families dearly.

I won't be making a big garden any more, but I still have a few cans of vegetables left for the family when they come by. It has taken me a long time to reach the age of ninety. Without all the good help I have had, I could not have made it this long.

On October 4, 2013, Alveta went to be with the Lord, and when my time comes, I will meet her in heaven. Meanwhile, I will live alone with the knowledge that it won't be a long time until then, and I am ready when that time comes. And, as I am sitting and writing today, another one of our family has passed away. My brother-in-law, Howard Dotson at age 93 just went to be with the Lord, joining his wife, Edith, who passed away a few years ago. He will be missed by his family and friends.

I am all alone now, but I have had a good long life with Alveta (almost 69 years). We always lived our life with our children the way we wanted them to live with their families. I am thankful for being blessed with a long and happy life and with a Godly wife. We worked together, with each one looking out for the other and our family. We had a long happy life that the Lord blessed us with. The Lord granted Alveta her last wish: she wanted to go to heaven before me and quickly, and when my time comes I wish for the same, if it's God's will.

I hope our children and their children will understand how things were during the ninety years of my life. Alveta and I were happy growing a garden, canning vegetables, and making the jellies for our children and grandchildren. Both of us have loved them all dearly — I can't say in words how much.

My Family Tree

My Family Tree (Part 1)

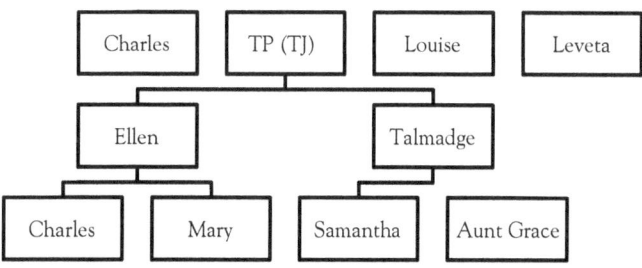

My Family Tree (Part 2)

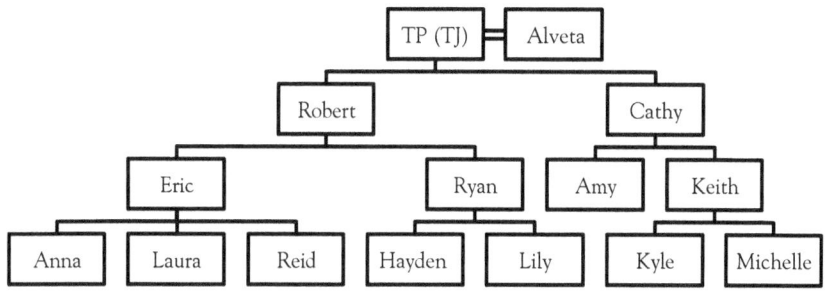

My Grandpa, Charles Pressley

My Grandma, Mary Elizabeth Putnam Pressley, & her brother, Wilson Putnam

My Mom, Ellen Pressley Fletcher

Alveta Medford

Charles & Me

Back: Left to Right — Charles Campbell (my sister Louise's husband), Alveta, & Jimmy Campbell.
Front: Left to Right — Cathy (my daughter) & Wanda Campbell in front of my house, 1962.

Memories from Thickety

Me leading the singing at church

Alveta and me at "Ghost Town"

Snow at our house, May 7-9, 1992

Alveta and me

Howard and Edith Dotson (Alveta's sister)

Hugh & Jennie Mae Early (Alveta's sister)

Hugh & Jennie Mae Early in Las Vegas

Alveta, Edith, & Jennie Mae

My son Robert, me, Robert's children, Ryan and Eric

My grandson Eric and his children, Anna, Reid, and Laura

Robert's family. Rear L-R: Ryan, his wife Robyn, their son Hayden, Diane and Robert, Eric's wife Maria and Eric, and their three children. Front L-R: Reid, Anna, and Laura

Eric's Family. Exchange student, Laura, Anna, Reid, Eric, and Maria

Ryan, Lily, and Hayden at the fair in 2010

Hayden and Lily

Cathy's family in the early 1990s

My grandson, Keith 1997

My granddaughter, Amy, Christmas 2010

My grandson, Keith
& his wife, Tara;

Keith, Tara & Kyle 2010

Great Grandson Kyle

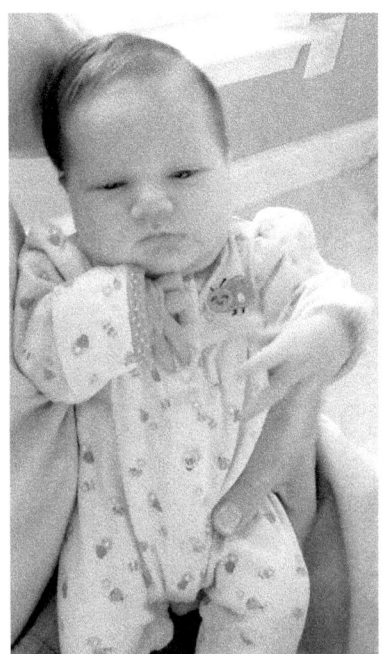
Keith & Tara's daughter
Michelle, 2013

Alveta & Great Grandson
Kyle, 2010

Keith & Tara's children,
Kyle and Michelle, 2013

Granddaughter Amy with her
niece Michelle, October 2013

Hugh and Jennie Mae's Children:
Ricky, Darlene, and Tommy

Me and my nephew,
Gary Fletcher, 2007,
with my house behind us

Family Christmas picture, 2008
Front, L-R: Grandson Keith, his wife Tara, Granddaughter Amy, and Cathy's husband, Jeff
Back, L-R: Alveta, me, son Robert, his wife Diane, and daughter Cathy

My nephew Gary, my son Robert, me, and my nephew Dean, October 2013

A few days after my 90th Birthday and a few days before my son-in-law Jeff's 62nd birthday, at my granddaughter Amy's house in October 2013

Me and my great-granddaughter Michelle, Thanksgiving, 2013

Acknowledgements

I would like to thank Amy DeWeese, my granddaughter, and Gary Fletcher, my nephew, for editing *Memories from Thickety*. I would also like thank my brother and publisher, Charles Fletcher, for his help and encouragement during the writing of this book.